millennium@drumshee

Drumshee Timeline Series
Book 7

Cora Harrison

Illustrated by Aileen Caffrey

WOLFHOUND PRESS

First published in 1999 by
Wolfhound Press Ltd
68 Mountjoy Square
Dublin 1, Ireland
Tel: (353-1) 874 0354
Fax: (353-1) 872 0207

 The Arts Council
An Chomhairle Ealaíon
Wolfhound Press receives financial assistance from The Arts
Council/An Chomhairle Ealaíon, Dublin, Ireland.

British Library Cataloguing in Publication Data
A catalogue record for this book is available from the British Library.

ISBN 0-86327-715-2

10 9 8 7 6 5 4 3 2 1

Cover illustration: Marie-Louise Fitzpatrick
Cover Design: Sally Mills-Westley
Typesetting: Wolfhound Press
Printed and bound by The Guernsey Press Co., Guernsey, Channel Islands

millennium@drumshee

Drumshee Timeline Series
Book 7

Cora Harrison taught primary-school children in England for twenty-five years before moving to a small farm in Kilfenora, Co. Clare. The farm includes an Iron Age fort, with the remains of a small castle inside it, and the mysterious atmosphere of this ancient place gave Cora the idea for a series of historical novels tracing the survival of the ringfort through the centuries. *millennium@drumshee* follows *Nuala & her Secret Wolf*, *The Secret of the Seven Crosses*, *The Secret of Drumshee Castle*, *The Secret of 1798*, *The Famine Secret* and *Titanic — Voyage from Drumshee* in the Drumshee Timeline Series.

For Edel Barry of Kilfenora,
Sophie Mason of London,
and my nephew Anthony Mockler of Sydney,
all of whom helped me with this book.
And with many thanks to my courageous and enthusiastic editor,
Eilís French of Wolfhound Press.

OTHER TITLES BY CORA HARRISON

Nuala & her Secret Wolf
Drumshee Timeline Series Book 1

The Secret of the Seven Crosses
Drumshee Timeline Series Book 2

The Secret of Drumshee Castle
Drumshee Timeline Series Book 3

The Secret of 1798
Drumshee Timeline Series Book 4

The Famine Secret
Drumshee Timeline Series Book 5

Titanic — Voyage from Drumshee
Drumshee Timeline Series Book 6

CHAPTER ONE

It was a hot night, too hot for sleep. For the twentieth time, Emma kicked off the bedclothes. She got up, opened the French window of her bedroom and stepped outside into the garden. Her bare toes curled away from the heat of the concrete path outside the new extension to the ancient stone cottage of Drumshee. She could hear the drone of an aeroplane coming in towards Shannon Airport, and the gurgle of the River Fergus at the bottom of the hill.

She leaned against the wall and closed her eyes. For a moment, she almost dozed.

Then her eyes jerked open as she heard her own name. They were talking about her again. Did they ever stop?

'The trouble with Emma is that she's spoilt,' came her father's voice, irritable as usual. 'I suppose it's because she's an only child. She has everything we can give her. There's not a child in the place has what she has — her own laptop computer, her own television, stereo, everything. And she does nothing but moan and sulk.'

Emma bit her thumbnail, savagely trying to tear it into a smooth oval, while she strained her ears to hear her mother's reply. It must have been some sort of defence, because her father sounded more exasperated than ever.

'It's no good you trying to excuse her behaviour, Joyce. I know she misses her friends in England, but why can't she make new friends here in Ireland? She's only twelve years old. There are lovely children here, far nicer than that gang she used to hang about with back in England. They're great kids, well-mannered, hard-working — I bet you'd never hear them say they're bored; they're too busy helping on the farms. Emma does nothing; she doesn't even help you much. She's just plain spoilt. We got her that dog because she wanted a German shepherd, and now she doesn't even train it. It's getting to be a thorough nuisance.'

Cautiously Emma closed the door and got back into bed. She didn't want to hear any more. She had heard it all already.

All her life, she had known that her father dreamed of going back to Drumshee, the home of his great-great-grandmother Deirdre. Now that his dream had come true, he didn't want anyone to interfere with his happiness.

It's all very well for him, Emma thought, kicking her duvet to the bottom of the bed. He's happily working away at his computer business; in his work, it doesn't matter whether he's in London or buried in the west of Ireland. But he's not going to force me to pretend I like this place.

She reached down to the basket beside her bed and touched Heidi's golden head. That had been the bribe her parents had offered her: a dog of her own. For ages, Emma had wanted a German shepherd, but she had always known that it was impossible — you couldn't keep a big dog in a London flat. So when Steve and Joyce Mantel had bought the little farm, Emma had asked for a puppy. Her parents had agreed, hoping to cheer her up.

In spite of her gloom, Emma smiled to herself as she remembered how gorgeous Heidi had been, that first day, when they had gone to choose her at the kennels in East Sussex. The dog breeder had been a very bossy lady who had tried to convince them that a small, quiet, timid puppy was the one they should choose; but the moment Emma saw Heidi, she had known that this funny, excitable, adorable, fluffy black puppy was the one she wanted.

'You might find her a bit of a handful,' the dog breeder had said thoughtfully, watching Heidi clambering on top of her brothers and sisters, still trying to get into Emma's arms, as the puppies were being shut away.

'What do you think, Joyce? Should we go for the small one instead?'

'Well, I'm not sure, but I think Emma should decide. After all, it will be her dog.'

'Well, you have a couple of weeks to think about it,' the dog breeder had said. 'They won't be ready to leave their mother for another two weeks.'

But Emma hadn't needed to think about it. She had christened the puppy Heidi and dreamed about her all through the last two weeks of term. Thinking about her had even made the good-byes bearable.

Heidi turned in her basket and twitched in her sleep, her little legs making running movements as if she were hunting rabbits in her dream. Emma got out of bed again, knelt on the floor beside Heidi and laid her cheek against the silky fur.

She's so beautiful, Emma thought. She's the most beautiful dog in the world.

As Heidi had grown, her back had stayed black — no longer fluffy, but a sleek, shining black — while her underside and her legs had turned the palest gold. Her face was golden too, except for a delicate pencilling of black around her glowing amber eyes. Her looks were perfect; if only her behaviour were perfect as well!

CHAPTER TWO

Emma slept badly that night, and the next morning she could see in her mirror that she had black shadows under her eyes. Carefully she licked the tip of her pencil and smudged a bit more black under them. Now I look really ill, she thought. Maybe Mum and Dad will start to feel sorry for me — maybe they'll even think about going back to London and buying a house with a garden, where I could see my friends again and still have Heidi ....

At the thought, she saw in the mirror that the colour had rushed into her normally pale cheeks. I'll take Heidi for a run down to the river before breakfast, she thought. I don't want to go in to breakfast looking too healthy.

The air was still hot, but it was damp and heavy with moisture. Emma was sweating when she came into the kitchen. She poured out Heidi's food and sat down at the table.

Her father stared at her in annoyance. 'You'd think that at your age you'd be able to wash your face before you come to breakfast,' he said. 'You've got black smears all under your eyes.'

'Sorry,' mumbled Emma, scrubbing at her cheeks.

'Was it nice down by the river?' asked her mother with forced brightness.

'No,' said Emma glumly, taking the packet of Weetabix down from the dresser. 'It was sticky and horrible and there were midges everywhere.'

She rather hoped that would start an argument; she felt just in the mood for a fight. But from the corner of her eye she saw her mother give her father a warning glance, and nothing was said.

Something was going to be said, though. Emma could feel it in the air. She knew her mother was going to announce something and was just waiting until Emma was in a better mood.

Defiantly, she kept her eyes fixed on the tablecloth and half-listened to the radio. The Irish economy of the late 90s was better than it had ever been, announced the unseen voice with its alien accent. Emma scowled even more. She knew all about this wonderful Irish economic boom. If it weren't for that, her father would probably still be working in London and she would still be happy ....

She pushed her plate away and stood up. 'I'd better be getting ready for school,' she muttered.

'Wait a minute,' said her mother nervously. 'Last night, I telephoned that nice woman in the shop in Kilfenora and asked if Róisín and Aisling would like to come and have tea with you today. I hope that was all right.'

Emma stared at her in horror. 'You did what?' she said. 'Oh, no. I'm not going to school today. You can say I'm sick. I am, anyway — I'm sick of that school! I hate it and I hate all of them and they hate me. They don't want to come to tea with me. They'll think I'm mental, anyway, if my mother has to go around inviting people to come and play with me as if I were three years old.'

'Don't speak to your mother like that,' said her father. 'You should be grateful. She goes to a lot of trouble for you — she was up until midnight making cakes for you and your friends to have today, and now she has to go off to work. Why are you upsetting her?'

'No one cares about upsetting me!' cried Emma. 'Why can't you leave me alone?' She dug her nails into her hands to stop the tears coming. She was always crying these days.

She looked at her mother defiantly, and was horrified to see tears in Joyce's eyes as well.

'Oh, all right,' she said hastily. 'I'm sorry, Mum. It won't work out, but I'll be polite to them, since you've arranged it.'

Without waiting for any more comments, Emma fled to her bedroom and washed her face. I suppose I'm lucky in some ways, she thought glumly. My own study-bedroom, my own bathroom, everything I could want — everything except friends and familiar places .... Hastily she pulled on jeans, a cropped top and a clean sweatshirt — it still felt funny not to have a school uniform — dragged a comb through her silky blond hair, got her school-bag and went back into the kitchen. Her father had disappeared into his study, she was glad to see. She hoped that he would remember to take Heidi out at lunch-time, and that he wouldn't shout at her too much.

'Be good,' she said, bending down and rubbing the soft hair behind the dog's ears. It was funny: Heidi always knew when Emma was going to school, and never tried to join her.

'It'll soon be the summer holidays, anyway,' she said as she took her place beside her mother in the battered old Metro.

'Do you really not like school, then?' said Joyce, as she turned the car and bumped down the uneven avenue.

Emma looked at her in exasperation. Did parents ever listen? She had said a million times that she hated school! She opened her mouth, and then closed it again. What was the point? Her mother had a hard day ahead of her, working in the hospital in Ennis.

'Stop by the gate, Mum,' she said. 'I want to check the letter-box.'

Her mother sighed. 'Emma, you know you went down twice yesterday evening, and the post doesn't come until four o'clock,' she said.

Emma frowned impatiently and drummed her fingers on the dashboard. Her mother stopped the car, and Emma got out and peered into the letter-box. Nothing there. She turned away, then went back and opened the letter-box fully, in case she had missed a small envelope lying at the bottom. But no, it was definitely empty.

Emma's heart felt sore. She had written so many letters to all of her friends, and now they seemed to have given up replying. She had been forgotten. They probably never even talked about her any more. Even at the chess tournaments where she had been a star — the pride of her school, one of the best girl chess-players ever in south-west London — she would only be remembered as last year's winner, and soon even that would be forgotten. With her lips set tightly together, she got back into the car and slammed the door.

As soon as she arrived at school, Emma saw Róisín and Aisling in the playground, near the gate.

They were talking to some other girls, and from the embarrassed looks they gave Emma she knew that they had been talking about her. With her face set rigidly and her eyes looking straight ahead, she passed them without a word.

She went into the classroom and dropped into her seat. There was no one else there; there wasn't even a computer behind which she could hide her loneliness. She took out her Irish book and pretended to study it. She hadn't a clue what it was all about; the only thing she knew for certain was that a word was never, ever, pronounced in the same way as it was spelt.

Apart from Irish, lessons weren't too bad, and the teacher was nice. The real ordeal was play-time. Emma had given up talking to the other girls; they seemed shy of her, almost embarrassed, when she talked to them about London and her old school. No one played chess; all of them, girls and boys, played a strange sort of football which Emma hated. The only thing she could do was sit in the classroom and read a book. And she couldn't even do that in peace — one of the teachers was always hounding her out to get some fresh air.

On her way out to the playground, Aisling stopped by Emma's desk.

'Are we coming to your house after school?' she asked.

Emma raised her eyes from her book with a look of pretended surprise. 'I suppose so,' she said. 'That's if you want to, of course.'

Aisling looked a bit confused. 'Your mam asked my mam,' she said.

'That's OK, then,' said Emma. Aisling, she noticed, had not said that she wanted to. She would probably hate it.

She looked at Aisling's troubled face and began to feel a little ashamed of herself.

'You can see my puppy,' she said, with an effort. 'She's just six months old. She's sweet.'

Aisling, Emma observed with a sinking heart, didn't seem very excited about that.

'I'm a bit scared of dogs,' she confessed. 'But I suppose if it's only a puppy, I won't mind it too much.'

Please yourself, thought Emma, and returned to her book.

'Are you coming out to play?' asked Aisling.

'No. I hate football,' said Emma briefly. She kept her eyes fixed on her book until she heard the classroom door close.

CHAPTER THREE

There was still an awkward silence between Emma, Aisling and Róisín as they turned in at the gate to Drumshee. They were halfway up the avenue before Aisling broke the silence.

'Do you like it here in Ireland?'

You've asked that twice already, Emma thought — and then a storm of barking broke out from the top of the hill. To Emma's horror, Heidi came flying down the avenue, barking wildly, the hackles on her back standing up as she tried to chase away the two intruders. Aisling screamed and began to run down the avenue; Róisín stood her ground for a moment and then followed her sister.

'Stand still,' yelled Emma. 'She won't hurt you! Heidi, come back, you bad dog!'

It was no good. Heidi had no intention of coming back; she had decided to get rid of these intruders. She raced ahead of the two terrified girls and turned to face them. She was barking wildly. With a feeling of sick despair, Emma suddenly realised that she was not at all sure that Heidi wouldn't attack.

'Heidi!' Emma screamed again. But when had Heidi ever done what she was told?

'Heidi,' yelled her father, coming thundering down the avenue with his old reading-glasses, which he used for computer work, sliding down his nose.

At that moment, the green post-office van turned in at the gate and drove up the avenue. The postman,

Mr Nolan, stopped just behind Heidi and blew his horn with a violence which made Heidi look around in alarm. Quick as a flash, he jumped out of the van, grabbed Heidi by the collar, lifted her off her front paws and shook her.

'Oh, don't hurt her,' cried Emma.

'It'll just teach her manners,' said Mr Nolan. 'That's the way the mother dog trains her pups. This is going to be a big dog; you can't have her running around doing whatever she likes.' He gave Heidi a final shake and set her down, still keeping a firm grip on her collar. To Emma's amazement, Heidi wagged her tail and even licked Mr Nolan's hand.

'Ah, you know who's boss, don't you?' he said.

Emma's father skidded to a halt and searched his pockets for his other glasses.

'I'm most grateful to you,' he said. 'I don't know what got into the dog. She's only a puppy, but she's getting out of hand. I hope she isn't turning savage. Emma, tell your friends how sorry you are.'

Emma winced. 'Sorry about all that,' she said awkwardly, feeling like a fool. 'Are you all right?'

Aisling tried to nod, but she couldn't stop crying. Róisín clung to her, sobbing.

'Come on, you two,' said Mr Nolan cheerfully. 'There's no harm done. She didn't bite you, did she? She was just barking.'

'Come up to the house and have some tea,' said Steve. 'You'll feel better then.'

'I want to go home,' wailed Róisín. 'I want to go home. I don't want any tea.'

'I think we'd better go home,' said Aisling, drying her eyes. 'We'll come another day,' she added hurriedly.

Chapter Three

Bet you don't, thought Emma, but she said nothing.

'I'll take them back,' said Mr Nolan. 'I'll be passing their house on my round.'

Their tears dried up quickly enough once they were safely inside the post-office van, thought Emma. They avoided her gaze when they saw her looking at them. She turned her back and went drearily up the avenue, holding Heidi by the collar. She went into her room and locked the door. Then she drew the curtains, threw herself on her bed and began to cry.

Heidi put her front paws on the bed and licked Emma's face consolingly. Emma cried all the more. With a sudden leap, Heidi got up on the bed and snuggled against her. She was strictly forbidden to get on the bed, but what did it matter now? Emma was terribly afraid that her father would try to get rid of Heidi. He really didn't like dogs; he had only given in to please his wife.

I'm not coming out until Mum comes home, thought Emma. I suppose Dad's ringing her at the hospital and telling her all about what happened. Emma knew that her mother would be upset, but she would be fair; she would know it hadn't been Emma's fault. But would she understand about Heidi? Maybe she too would think that Heidi should be given away .... At that thought, Emma sobbed even harder. She began to choke, and her breath started coming in great sobbing gasps.

She began to panic. I'm going to die, she thought. She staggered to her feet and unlocked the door. She didn't have enough breath left to call her father, but Heidi ran ahead of her, whining.

Steve was in the kitchen, with the telephone in his hand. He took one look at Emma, yelled, 'Oh my God, Joyce,' and dropped the phone and put his arm around her. Emma could vaguely hear her mother's voice coming from the dangling receiver. She tried to get her breath, but she could only gasp.

Steve snatched up the phone again.

'Joyce,' he said, 'I don't know what's wrong with Emma. Listen to her — she can't breathe! She's just gasping.' He held the receiver against Emma's mouth. To her relief, she heard her mother's voice.

'Emma, don't worry about a thing,' Joyce was saying. 'You've just got yourself upset. You'll be all right in a moment. Just take long, deep breaths. Let me talk to your dad, now, like a good girl. Don't worry, I'll be home soon. I'm just finishing my shift.' She raised her voice. 'Steve, are you there?'

Steve took the receiver. Emma concentrated on breathing slowly and deeply. After all, her mother was a nurse; she must know. Steve was saying, 'Yes ... yes ....' and 'A paper bag?' Then he put the phone down, rummaged in the drawer of the dresser and produced a crumpled paper bag.

'Breathe into this, Emma,' he said. 'That's what your mother says. Breathe slowly, and try to hold each breath as long as you can.'

Emma tried to breathe slowly. Her heart was still thudding wildly, but she was beginning to feel less panicky. Her mother had sounded quite calm; and even her father, a born fusser, was becoming less agitated. Perhaps she wasn't going to die, after all. If she were, her mother would have sent an ambulance. She managed to hold her breath for about ten seconds;

then she let it out and took another breath of the stale air from the paper bag.

'Good girl,' said her father. 'Now try to hold your breath while I count up to twenty.'

Emma blew out, a long slow breath that filled the paper bag so that it swelled like a balloon. Heidi reached up and patted it with a curious paw. Emma laughed and began to feel much better. She leaned against the back of the chair. It seemed wonderful just to be able to breathe normally again. She closed her eyes. She felt very tired.

'Come and lie on your bed,' said her father. 'Just slip off your shoes and get in under the covers. I'll make you a nice cup of tea.'

Emma lay down. She didn't really want any tea, but she lacked the energy to tell him.

When she woke up a couple of hours later, the cup of tea was there, quite cold, beside her bed. Hastily she poured it down the sink and went into the kitchen with her empty cup. Her mother was home from work. Emma could hear the voices in the kitchen. Talking about me, she thought wearily as she opened the door.

Luckily Heidi made a big fuss of her, jumping up and making little sounds of pleasure as if she hadn't seen Emma for weeks. Emma bent over her, stroking her, and avoided looking at her parents.

'I'll make us all a cup of tea,' said Steve, jumping up and bustling around the sink.

He's as embarrassed as I am, thought Emma. She sat down at the table and met her mother's eyes.

'I hear Heidi was a bit of a pain today,' said Joyce. 'We'll have to get you some help with training her.'

Chapter Three

Emma nodded silently. She was overwhelmed with relief that they hadn't said that Heidi must be given away.

'I'm sure she'll be fine,' said her mother briskly. 'She's a lovely dog, really; she's just going through a pre-teenage phase when she thinks she can have her own way in everything.'

Emma nodded again. Her cheeks felt a bit hot. Maybe I'm a bit like Heidi, she thought. Maybe I do want things my own way all the time.

'It's not Heidi we're worried about,' Joyce went on. 'We both feel bad that you're so unhappy. We've been talking about what we can do to make you happier, but we can't do anything if you won't talk to us and tell us how we can help.'

'What's the worst thing about living in Drumshee?' asked Steve, putting a steaming mug of tea in front of Emma.

Emma sipped the tea. It was too hot and it burned her tongue, but she wanted to give herself time to think. Both her parents were looking at her expectantly. She would have to say something. She searched her mind.

'I think it's the chess,' she said eventually. 'I really miss the chess. I would have been in the English junior team, this summer, and I would have been top girl junior, and ....' $537,694$

That was the right thing to say, she thought with satisfaction. Her father was looking contrite, almost ashamed.

'I know, I know,' he said hurriedly. 'We must find a club for you. It's a shame that no one around here plays. Perhaps we could start a chess club, the two of us. What about that? Tutor up some of the local kids and have a Kilfenora club — what would you think of that?'

Emma nodded languidly. She was too tired to argue. In any case, it was nice having him be so friendly for a change.

Steve looked at her uneasily. Even he could not convince himself that this would be a solution.

Then his face brightened.

'I've got it,' he said. 'What about the Internet? All sorts of people from all over the world play chess on the Internet. You could find someone of your own age and your own standard, and that would keep your chess up until the competitions start again in the winter.'

Emma tried to look pleased. She couldn't explain that it wasn't just the chess itself she enjoyed. She couldn't explain the excitement she'd felt when the school chess team had travelled all over England — the nail-biting tensions, the triumphs, the congratu- lations, the sheer fun the six team members had had.

She smiled, remembering the day of the Junior Championship in London. Their team had been given a nursery classroom for their home base, and while they were in the middle of eating their sand- wiches, Alex had suddenly pressed the 'ring' button on the toy telephone, picked it up, listened intently, and then handed it to Emma, saying seriously, 'It's the Teletubbies for you. They want to know if you can come out to play.' Somehow, it had seemed so funny that they had all laughed until their sides ached; and then, still laughing, they had gone in to play the final game of the Championship. Later, going home in the minibus, triumphantly waving the silver cup at all the cars behind, they had made up stupid songs about chess-playing Teletubbies. Even after all those months, the memory was enough to make her laugh again.

'Well, I can see you like the idea of that,' said Steve buoyantly. 'Let's go into your bedroom and put a notice on the Internet, before you change your mind.'

Emma was used to the Internet. When her father had first got it, in London, all her friends had come around and they had had a great time surfing the Net. She hadn't used it since they'd moved to Ireland, though. She had gradually lost interest in it.

She typed her message and put in her chess grade.

'You'll need an e-mail address,' said her father. 'Don't use your own name; it's never a good idea to put your own name on the Internet. Make up something, and I'll ring the server and make sure the address is set up and working by the time any replies come in. What would you like to call yourself?'

Emma thought for a moment and then filled in the address:

```
depressed@drumshee.ie
```

It looked cool, she thought.

CHAPTER FOUR

The next morning, when she came back from giving Heidi her run, Emma switched on her computer. At least it makes a change from walking down to the letter-box, she thought sourly. Of course, there was even less chance of finding anything. If her own friends couldn't be bothered to write to her, there wasn't much chance of a stranger replying.

But she was wrong. There it was, waiting for her in her in-box. Hands trembling with excitement, Emma opened the message.

```
From:        bruce.mcm@clubi.com.au
To:          depressed@drumshee.ie
```

Drumshee? Believe it or not, my great-great-grandfather came from a place called Drumshee, in Ireland, in County Clare. Where is your Drumshee? And why are you depressed, anyway? No, don't tell me. I'm pretty depressed myself. I don't want to hear anyone else's troubles. Let's play chess.

I hope you don't mind, but I've played the first four moves for us and we can carry on from there. It'll save time. Of course, I don't know how much time you've got. I've all the time in the world, myself, but you mightn't be so lucky — or so unlucky. Anyway, here goes:

```
1       e2 - e4              e7 - e5
2       g1 - f3              b8 - c6
3       f1 - b5              g8 - f6
4       0 - 0
```

(I know, I know — boring old Ruy Lopez, but what the hell, let's not be original!)

Emma clicked on 'Reply' and began typing without even stopping to think.

From: depressed@drumshee.ie
To: bruce.mcm@clubi.com.au

OK, OK, bossy, let's try your pathetic old opening. You don't say how old you are, but I suppose you must be about ninety to be still using Ruy Lopez. Thanks for playing my part of the game, anyway. I'm sure I could never have thought of anything so original! :-)

Anyway, my next move is:

4   d7 - d6

You'll notice that I'm not falling into your nice little trap!

Funnily enough, my Drumshee is in County Clare, so maybe it's the place where your great-great-grandfather came from. My great-great-grandmother came from here too, as a matter of fact, and that's why my father bought this place — that and the fact that Ennis, our nearest so-called big town, is an Information Age Town.

Anyway, we moved over here from London a few months ago. My name is Emma Mantel, and I'm twelve years old. Here are some questions for you:

1. How old are you?

2. What part of Australia do you come from?

3. Why are you depressed? (I think I *would* like to know why other people get depressed. It must be my lovely nature :-).)

Emma sent off the message and then went into the kitchen. She was the first up, so she put the kettle on and, humming an Oasis song, began to set the table.

'You're cheerful this morning,' said her mother, coming in yawning, her hair still damp from the shower.

'After breakfast, you must have a look and see if you've had any replies on the Net,' said Steve, following Joyce in and pouring himself a cup of tea.

'I have,' said Emma smugly. 'And I've written back to him. It's someone called Bruce in Australia. I don't know what sort of a chess player he is, though. He didn't give his grade. Believe it or not, he's using the Ruy Lopez.'

'Well, I don't know,' began her father. 'I often use the Ruy Lopez myself.'

'Yes, but, Dad, you're way out of date. When did you last play competitive chess?' said Emma impatiently.

'Now then,' said her father good-humouredly, 'don't forget who taught you chess. I remember a time when you thought a fool's mate was the most brilliant chess sequence ever invented.'

Emma laughed.

She felt much happier all that morning. It felt like such a long time since the previous day that it gave her a shock when, during the morning break, the fat dark girl with the name Emma could never pronounce said to her with a sneer, 'I hear you've got a powerful wicked dog at Drumshee.'

Emma flushed. She hated anyone to criticise Heidi. She had been thinking about going out to the playground — in fact, she had already risen from her chair — but she sat down again and hastily got a book out from her desk.

'Don't be horrible,' said Orla Nolan, the postman's daughter. 'My dad says she's a beautiful dog. She just needs a bit of training, he said.'

To her horror, Emma felt her eyes fill with tears.

'Thanks,' she said awkwardly, and looked down at her book.

Orla, however, did not go away. She sat down beside Emma.

'I love dogs, don't you?' she said chattily. 'We've got eight of them.'

'Eight!' Emma was so astonished that the book fell from her hands. She giggled. 'I wonder what my dad would say about that. He moans enough about having one, about her hair getting on the floor and about her barking at night.'

'My dad loves dogs,' Orla said. 'He's promised me a dog of my own for my birthday, next week. I'm going to have a springer spaniel. He's four months old. Do you want to come and see him when he comes?'

'I'd love to,' said Emma. She thought about asking Orla if she would like to come and see Heidi. But what if Heidi behaved the way she had with Róisín and Aisling?

'Four months is quite old for a puppy to be leaving home, isn't it?' she said, hoping that the conversation was going to go on. 'Heidi was only two months old when I got her.'

'Well, you see,' said Orla, in a whisper, 'this dog was very bad. He kept running away and chasing sheep, and the owners were going to have him shot, but my father said he would take him. He's going to help me train him. Don't tell anyone, though, will you? It's supposed to be a secret, because the man who owns him now promised the farmer that he'd have him put down.'

'I promise,' Emma whispered back.

A warm feeling crept into her. Perhaps, after all, she might make friends with some of the others at school. They had been very nice when she first arrived, she had to admit to herself; but she had been so miserable, and had missed all her friends in England so much, that she hadn't wanted to make friends with any of them.

Emma came home from school that day feeling almost happy. Orla had been friendly to her all day long, and she was looking forward to seeing whether there was a message on her computer from that Australian boy.

She dumped her school-bag on the ground, called out a cheerful 'hello' to her father, who was tapping away at his computer in his study, hugged Heidi, pulled on her wellies and climbed up the steep bank towards the *cathair* — the ancient fort behind the cottage. Heidi raced ahead, carrying her favourite pink rubber bone in her mouth.

Emma always liked going into the *cathair*. It was completely surrounded by old blackthorn bushes, and when you stepped into it you felt as if you were in another world. History was Emma's favourite subject at school, and she always felt a slight thrill when she went into the *cathair* and imagined people from Iron Age times, two thousand years ago, living and working on the very spot where she stood. She could almost imagine a girl of her own age standing there, in the very same place ....

She paused for a few minutes, holding Heidi's bone in her hand and peering through the thick canopy of leaves, trying to see into the past. Then she turned around to throw the bone for Heidi. But Heidi was gone.

'Heidi!' Emma yelled, looking around. How could the dog have vanished so quickly? She was nowhere to be seen. Emma ran out of the *cathair*, into the little Cathaireen Field. Heidi wasn't there either.

A cold feeling came over Emma. Her father's warning words came into her mind:

'Never let her wander,' he had said. 'If she gets in amongst sheep, any farmer will shoot her. You can't blame them. It's their livelihood. And once a dog starts chasing sheep, it won't stop.'

Her heart hammering as if she had run for miles, Emma ran down the little lane to the flat piece of land, surrounded by a stream, which was always called the Isle of Maain.

'Heidi,' she screamed again and again, trying to force her legs to go faster. 'Heidi, you bad girl, come back! Heidi!'

She had almost reached the top of the little sunken lane when the sound she had been dreading reached her ears. It was the sound of sheep bleating — not just peaceful bleats, but wild, frightened, urgent explosions of sound. Emma felt as if her chest would burst, and she had a crippling stitch in her side, but she didn't dare stop to draw breath.

The sheep were up on the slopes, near a briar-filled old quarry. They were gathered together in a tight cluster, facing down the slope, and their alarmed bleating was so loud that Emma feared the farmer would arrive at any moment.

She stopped and stared around, gasping for breath, her heart thudding against her ribs. 'Heidi!' she screamed again.

Then, in a last despairing effort, she flung the rubber bone as hard as she could, so that it bounced and thudded on the springy grass.

'Heidi!' she shouted, making her voice as excited as she could. 'Seek your bone, Heidi!'

And then, as if a miracle had happened, there was a splashing sound from the little stream which ran along the side of the Isle of Maain. A golden head appeared, and Heidi raced across the grass and picked up the bright pink bone. She came running up, tail wagging, amber eyes gleaming with fun, and dropped the bone at Emma's feet.

'Oh, Heidi!' said Emma. She felt too weak to say anything else. In any case, she remembered reading that you should never scold a dog who has come back, no matter how long it has been missing.

She gripped Heidi's collar tightly and put the bone in her pocket.

'Come on, Heidi,' she said, with a frightened glance all around. There was no sign of the farmer. 'Let's get out of here before anyone sees you.'

It was hard work keeping hold of Heidi's collar. Really, thought Emma, she's getting too strong for me. Heidi was still very excited. She was panting heavily. She had obviously run a long distance, probably after a fox or a hare. Emma prayed hard that no one had seen her.

She didn't dare let go of the collar, even for an instant, in case Heidi took off again. By the time they got back to the cottage, her arm felt as if it had been pulled loose from its socket.

'Well,' said her father, meeting them at the porch, 'you both look as if you've been having a good time. Has Heidi been in the river?'

'She's had a paddle,' said Emma, trying to think what she could say if he asked any more.

Steve, however, wasn't really listening. 'Well,' he said, 'there's a message waiting for you from your young man in Australia. I was on-line to London myself and I saw it come in.'

'You didn't look, I hope,' said Emma teasingly, glad to move the conversation away from Heidi.

'Of course not. That address is yours and yours only. I'll fix it so that your mail only comes to your computer, if you like. I'd like to check out a few of the first messages, though, just to make sure that he's genuine.'

'OK,' said Emma. She didn't really care; there was nothing private about playing chess. However, she knew that her father loved tinkering with computers, so he would enjoy doing it.

'Well, I'll make us a couple of mugs of tea while you read your message,' he said. 'Your mother will be a bit late tonight, so I'll make us sandwiches as well, and then I'll check out your computer.'

Emma went into her room and switched on her laptop. She had been using computers since she was three years old, and by now it was second nature to her to move quickly through the Start menu and into her e-mail program.

From: bruce.mcm@clubi.com.au
To: depressed@drumshee.ie

You think you have something to be depressed about? What about me? You've probably got a great life. Here I am, lying on a hospital bed — St Mary's Hospital in Sydney, actually — with my right leg broken in three places. I'm in traction and I have to stay here for months. Luckily I've got my laptop with me, and the hospital's education programme has Internet access (I've kept my own e-mail address, though). Still, I'm going out of my mind with boredom; even surfing the Net loses its charm if you have nothing else to do for sixteen hours a day. Nothing this bad has happened to me in fourteen years (yes, you've guessed it — I'm fourteen, almost fifteen).

Anyway, write me a long letter and tell me anything to cheer me up or just to pass the time. Tell me all about Drumshee. My grandfather had a map on his wall, showing all the fields of Drumshee and their names. *His* grandfather Daniel drew it when he came out to Australia. I suppose he was homesick. All the names are in Irish, so I couldn't pronounce them for a million dollars. I remember them, though: An Cathair, Páirc Gharbh (which I think means Rough Field), An Cluain Mhór (the Big Meadow?), Páirc Togher and Cathairín — oh, and somewhere called the Isle of Maain.

By the way, I've changed my mind. Sheer boredom forces me to ask, very politely: why are you depressed? <yawn>

Anyway, my next chess move is (wait for it!):

5   d2 - d4

Bruce

Emma stared at the move for a moment. Then she went and set up her chessboard. That wasn't the move she had expected. Bruce might be a better chess player than she had imagined.

Her pulse quickened. This might be fun.

CHAPTER FIVE

It was great having an e-mail friend in Australia, Emma thought. It was lovely to wake up and find a message from the other side of the world waiting for you. Even before taking Heidi for her run, she logged on and checked her mail.

It was a really long letter this time.

```
From:        bruce.mcm@clubi.com.au
To:          depressed@drumshee.ie

I broke my stupid leg, as I told you, and
now I have to have another operation because
it isn't mending properly. So this will be
the last e-mail for a few days. Never mind,
it will give you time to think out a good
answer to my latest brainwave:

6    b1 - c3 (neat, eh?)

I think you're making too much fuss about
your dog and all the trouble you have with
her. She sounds great. Who cares about silly
old sheep, anyway? Personally, I hate lamb.
We seemed to eat nothing else when I was
little. I'd like to see a photograph of your
dog. I suppose you'd have to send it by
silly old snail mail, though, unless you
have a scanner.

Now, here comes Brainwave Number Two. Why
don't you ask that girl Orla if the two of
you can train your dogs together? Two kids I
know used to do that. They were training gun
dogs, and they used to go to the beach here
in Sydney every morning, before school, and
work with their dogs. They had a great time,
```

and they were always going in for competitions
and things and trying to do better than each
other.

What does your father do, and how could he
just move from London to the west of Ireland?
And what's all this about Ennis being an
Information Age Town? I haven't a clue what
you're talking about. My father is a bank
manager (I know, boring!). He used to get
moved around when I was young, but now he'll
stay in Sydney, which is OK by me. Sydney is
great — at least, it's great if you're not
stuck in a hospital bed.

Send me an e-mail before midnight (your
time) and then I'll get it before they wheel
me in for the butchers to have a bit of
knife practice on me.

Emma took a long breath. That gave her something
to think about.

She moved Bruce's knight on the chessboard, and
wrote him a quick message.

```
From:       depressed@drumshee.ie
To:         bruce.mcm@clubi.com.au
```

Good luck with the operation. Here's something to worry you before you go in:

6   f8 - e7

She clicked her fingers at Heidi. I'll just take her
down the House Meadow, she decided. She didn't
want to risk going near the Isle of Maain again.

That was a really good idea of Bruce's, she thought.
I'll ask Orla today. After all, both their dogs had
problems; and perhaps Orla's father would work a
bit of magic on Heidi again, like he had on the day
when Róisín and Aisling had come to tea.

'Bruce is having an operation today,' Emma told her parents at breakfast. 'I think I'll make him a "Get Well Soon" card when I come back. Oh, and Dad, could I send him a photograph of Heidi? He said he'd like to see her.'

'No problem,' said her father, munching his toast. 'If you give me one, I'll scan it and have it ready for you when you come back from school. Then you can send it to him by e-mail. Why is he having an operation?'

'He broke his leg,' said Emma, getting up from the table and putting her plate and mug into the dishwasher. 'I'd better go. I'll walk, Mum. Take your time.'

As she walked down the road, Emma planned what she would say to Orla. She was pleased to see her waiting by the school fence.

'Hi,' said Orla, as soon as Emma got to the gate. 'My dad was saying last night that when I get Tinker — that's the puppy's name — maybe you and I can work together at training both of our dogs.'

'You'll never believe it,' said Emma, 'but I was going to say the exact same thing to you!'

'We must be telepathic,' said Orla.

'Well, to be honest, it wasn't my idea,' said Emma. 'This boy in Australia who I write to — he was the one who suggested it.'

'Is he your boyfriend?' asked Orla, enviously.

'Not really,' said Emma. 'I've never even met him. We have what's called a virtual relationship: we communicate over the Net. With our computers, I mean — over the Internet,' she added, seeing by Orla's blank face that she didn't understand.

'Have you got a computer?' asked Orla. 'I'd love to have a computer of my own. Mind you, I wouldn't know what to do with it if I did have one.'

'I'll show you, if you like,' offered Emma.

'Could I come and see your computer after school?' asked Orla eagerly. 'And Heidi, of course.'

'I suppose so,' said Emma doubtfully, feeling her heart sink a little.

'I won't stay for tea or anything,' said Orla. 'I know that your mam works. I'll just stay for a little while.'

'It's not that,' said Emma honestly. 'It's just that I'm afraid Heidi might rush up and bark at you, the way she did at Róisín and Aisling.'

'I'll tell you what,' said Orla. 'My dad will be delivering letters around here at about that time. We'll wait for him and go up with him. My dad is very good with dogs. They always do what he says.'

Emma smiled. 'Great,' she said.

It all worked like a dream. Emma and Orla drove up the avenue in Mr Nolan's van, both squashed together on the front seat. When they reached the cottage, Mr Nolan and Emma got out; Emma went indoors, fastened the lead to Heidi's collar, and brought her outside. Heidi began to bark, but when she saw the post-office van she changed her mind and wagged her tail instead.

'Get out of the van, Orla. Just take it easy and don't worry if she barks. Now, Emma, as soon as she barks, hold the lead tightly and shout "No" as crossly as you can. Let her see that she mustn't behave like that. I'll help you if she pulls, but you must be the one who's cross with her.'

As soon as Heidi gave one bark, Emma managed to let out a very fierce-sounding 'No!' Heidi rocked back in surprise and looked at Emma quite meekly.

'Good girl, Heidi,' Emma said.

'Well done, that's the way — always praise your dog when she does something right. Now, Orla, you come up and make friends with her.'

Orla patted Heidi cautiously.

'I know what I'll do,' said Emma, handing the lead to Mr Nolan. 'I'll get her bone. She loves to play with it. If you throw it for her, Orla, she'll make great friends with you.'

As soon as the bright pink bone was brought out, Heidi whined with excitement. Orla threw the bone again and again, and again and again Heidi brought it back, tail wagging and amber eyes shining with excitement.

Orla's father watched with interest. 'You might make a very good dog out of that German shepherd,' he said to Emma. 'She's got it all, brains as well as beauty. I like the way she concentrates on finding that bone. Once you get her under control, you'll have a dog to be proud of. Well, I'd better go. People will be waiting for their letters. Do you want to come with me, Orla?'

'Oh, no — please, may she stay?' begged Emma. 'I promised to show her the Internet on my computer, and my dad will make us his super-duper sandwiches. Oh, here he comes. Dad, this is Orla, and you know Mr Nolan. It's OK if Orla stays for tea, isn't it?'

'Of course it is. I'm delighted. Nice to meet you. Sorry about not coming out earlier; I was on-line to London. I still do most of my business with London,

Chapter Five

although I'm beginning to build up here in Ireland. How is Heidi behaving herself?'

'Oh, she's grand, she's grand entirely,' said Mr Nolan easily. 'You work with computers, don't you? It must be very interesting.'

'Yes; I design databases for firms, and I'm also starting to be a specialist in security procedures for businesses.'

'Well, you've got the makings of a fine guard dog there.'

Steve laughed. 'I don't mean that sort of security. I mean stopping hackers and that sort of thing — you know, people who get access to private bank accounts, or to firms' private affairs, through their own computers.'

'You're losing me, I'm afraid. I don't know a thing about computers. I wish they would teach the kids something about them in school, though. The future will be computers, there's no doubt about that.'

'Well, perhaps we should do a bit of fund-raising and buy a couple of computers for the school. I know Emma misses having a computer in her classroom. In her school in London, all the kids had laptops.'

Oh no, thought Emma. Don't start organising everyone else's lives for them.

'Come and see my computer, Orla,' she said. 'It's in my bedroom.'

'Can Heidi come too?' asked Orla.

'Of course she can,' replied Emma, glowing with pride in her beautiful dog, who, for once, seemed to be behaving herself.

To Emma's surprise, there was a message waiting for her. It was from Bruce.

```
From:        bruce.mcm@clubi.com.au
To:          depressed@drumshee.ie

Delay at the Meat Factory. Just time to answer
your last mail.

7      f1 - e1 (Good, eh?)

Keep smiling.
```

'That's this Australian boy,' explained Emma. 'He's having an operation today. He broke his leg and it isn't mending, so he has to have another operation.'

'How did he break it?' asked Orla.

'I don't know. He didn't say.'

'Probably he was surfing. Just like in *Neighbours*,' said Orla.

They looked at each other with delight. It really does sound exciting, thought Emma.

CHAPTER SIX

From: bruce.mcm@clubi.com.au
To: depressed@drumshee.ie

Dear Emma,

Thanks for the 'Get Well' card. It was
great. Your computer art is really cool. One
of the first things I did when I stopped
feeling groggy after the operation was to
open my mailbox and read your message. I was
glad you didn't put in another chess move —
I wouldn't have been up to it. I must say,
you play pretty good chess.

That was great, the story about how Heidi
terrorised the parish priest. I laughed so
much that the nurse came in to see what was
the matter. She thought I was howling with
pain. I could just see it all. I suppose the
poor man prayed all the way back to Kilfenora.
Poor old Heidi — I suppose she's in the dog-
house again. Anyway, being a German, she
probably isn't a Catholic; she's probably a
Lutheran. Tell your dad that one.

Must stop now, I see a nurse advancing on me
with a sharp-pointed instrument. Mail me
again soon and tell me the latest details in
Heidi's life of crime.

All the best,

Bruce

Emma looked at her watch. She had just time to
reply before she had to go to school. Quickly she
keyed in her message.

From: depressed@drumshee.ie
To: bruce.mcm@clubi.com.au

There's no life of crime at the moment, I'm
glad to say. Dad was so upset about this
business with Heidi and the parish priest that
he pays Orla's father to give me a lesson
with Heidi every day. Orla comes too, and we
have a great time. She's getting her dog
next week, so we're hoping that Heidi and
Tinker will be great friends. Orla's dad
says that Heidi is very clever but very,
very strong-willed. He told my dad that
she's a very difficult dog for someone of my
age to handle and that I've done very well
with her. I was really pleased when he said
that, because I'd become used to thinking
that it was all my fault that she was doing
these terrible things.

I hope you're feeling better. Tell me when
you want to carry on playing chess.

By the way, my friend Orla wants to know
whether you broke your leg surfing. If you
did, tell us all about it.

Bruce's answer arrived the next morning, as Emma
was getting ready for school.

From: bruce.mcm@clubi.com.au
To: depressed@drumshee.ie

Dear Emma,

Stop signing yourself 'depressed'. You don't
sound a bit depressed any more.

Yes, I did break my leg surfing. Clever of
you to guess. I'm mad on surfing, and every
day after school all my crowd take our surf-
boards down to the sea. It's the greatest fun
on earth. There's always this exciting moment
when half of you is scared stiff and thinks
you're going to die, and the other half

thinks 'What the hell, it'll be worth it!'

I think I'm well enough to play chess again, so send me your next move. I have a bet on with my father about what move you'll make. He thinks one thing and I think something totally different, so I hope you do my one — it'll be worth two dollars to me if you do.

By the way, you still haven't told me what an Information Age Town is. It sounds like something out of Star Trek.

School had started by the time Emma came in, but it didn't matter. That was the nice thing about Irish schools: loads of people came in late from time to time, and no one seemed to take any notice. The teacher just gave Emma a nice smile as she slid into her seat next to Orla.

'He did break his leg surfing,' she whispered to Orla, as they all stood up to say the morning prayer.

'I bet he's really good-looking, really tanned,' Orla said as they sat down. 'Why don't you ask him over for a holiday? Our summer is his winter, so he might like to come then, in July.'

'I'd better get Heidi trained first, or else she might go for him the way she did for the priest,' giggled Emma, digging in her bag for her homework.

Over the next few weeks, Emma found herself enjoying school more and more. Everyone seemed to be friends with her now. But there was nothing she enjoyed more than the hour between five and six o'clock, when Orla, Mr Nolan, and little Tinker came over and they all went down to the Big Meadow for their dog-training class.

Tinker was inclined to run away, so they all practised running away from him as fast they could.

Long-legged Heidi effortlessly kept up with the two girls, while Tinker, with his short legs, had an awful time catching up with them.

'That's one thing about Heidi, anyway,' said Orla. 'She doesn't run away from you.'

'Yes, indeed,' agreed Mr Nolan. 'She's very devoted to you. You have a great relationship.'

Emma said nothing. She still didn't like to think about that terrible day when Heidi had run away from her and gone down to the Isle of Maain, amongst the sheep.

That evening she took Heidi to the House Meadow and practised the day's lesson over and over again. Heidi was getting quite good: she would walk on the lead without pulling Emma's arm from its socket, and she would actually lie down when she was told to.

When they were both tired, Heidi went into her basket and Emma wrote to Bruce. It was great having a friend in Australia. All the girls in school were really envious of her. And it was a great game of chess they were playing. It had been going on for weeks, and it was getting better all the time.

Emma took her chess notebook out of the drawer of her desk. She hadn't used it since she had left England, and it was lovely to be filling up another page.

She had written 'White: Bruce McMahon of Sydney, Australia,' on the first line, and 'Black: Emma Mantel of Drumshee, County Clare, Ireland,' on the second. She looked through the moves that they had already played and carefully filled them into her notebook. Then she arranged the pieces on her study position diagram. Alex had given her the stick-on chess pieces for her birthday the year before.

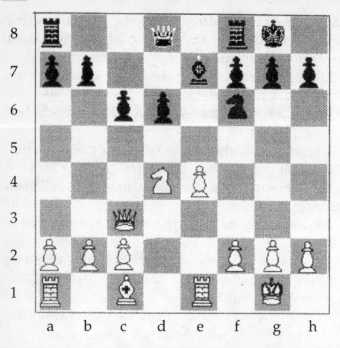

WHITE:	Bruce McMahon, Sydney, Australia
BLACK:	Emma Mantel, Drumshee, Co. Clare, Ireland

1	e2 - e4	e7 - e5
2	g1 - f3	b8 - c6
3	f1 - b5	g8 - f6
4	0 - 0	d7 - d6
5	d2 - d4	c8 - d7
6	b1 - c3	f8 - e7
7	f1 - e1	e5 x d4
8	f3 x d4	c6 x d4
9	d1 x d4	d7 x b5
10	c3 x b5	0 - 0
11	d4 - c3	c7 - c6
12	b5 - d4	

46

Chapter Six

Suddenly Emma realised that she hadn't thought about Alex, or any of her London friends, in a long time. They all seemed very young to her now.

She dismissed London from her thoughts and turned her mind to the chess game. 'B5 to d4,' she murmured to herself. That had been Bruce's last move.

After much thought, she wrote:

12   f6 - d7

Then she put her chess notebook away and went to the computer. She glanced through Bruce's old e-mails. He's right, she thought; I'm not depressed any more.

She opened the Settings file and changed her e-mail address.

```
From:      emma@drumshee.ie
To:        bruce.mcm@clubi.com.au

Dear Bruce,

Dog show on Saturday. Don't laugh, but I'm
going to try Heidi in an obedience class, if
she seems OK. I'm a bit worried about it,
but Orla and her dad are going as well, and
Heidi's always very well-behaved when Mr
Nolan is around. She loves him, but she's been
respectful towards him ever since the time
when he shook her. I wish I'd done something
like that the first time I met Heidi — but
then, I don't suppose I could ever have done
such a thing. She was so gorgeous — just a
little bundle of soft black fur.

I'm not too sure about this Information Age
Town business myself. I know it means that
every house in Ennis got a computer, all the
schools are connected to the Internet, every
telephone has voice mail, everyone in town
has electronic purses (little cards they use
```

to buy small things) — a whole lot of things like that. My dad is very excited about it. He says towns and cities all over the world will be looking to Ennis.

Anyway, here's my next chess move. Bet it takes you all day to work it out. Wait for it:

12   f6 - d7

Emma

CHAPTER SEVEN

Next morning Emma woke up to the sound of rain beating down on the corrugated-iron roof of the old stone cow cabin. 'No dog show today, Heidi,' she said aloud. Heidi wagged her tail vigorously, making a drumming sound on the side of the wardrobe.

'So you didn't want to go either,' said Emma. 'To be honest with you, Heidi, I was a bit nervous myself. You might have bitten the judge, and then we'd both have had to leave the country. Anyway, it's only half past seven and it's Sunday, so let's go back to sleep.'

When Emma woke up for the second time, the rain was still heavy. She pulled on her wellies and her wax jacket and went down through the soaking fields to where the little River Fergus, swollen by the night's rain, ran fast and furious under its stone bridge. There was a frog sitting on a stone, staring at the water; when Heidi nosed it, it began to take wild sideways leaps through the grass, followed by Heidi, jumping like a little kangaroo.

'Come back, you daft dog,' shouted Emma. To her surprise, Heidi returned to her side immediately.

'Good girl!' said Emma. She couldn't get used to Heidi doing what she was told. It seemed like a minor miracle every time she obeyed a command.

She stroked the wet fur on the top of the dog's golden head.

'Do you know, Heidi,' she said solemnly, 'you'll

never believe this, but I think I'm beginning to like this place, rain and all.'

'No dog show today,' said Steve, when Emma got back to the cottage. 'They'll be bound to cancel on a day like this.'

'I'll ring Orla after breakfast,' said Emma.

Orla was washing her hair when Emma rang, but Mr Nolan was amused at the idea that the show might be cancelled.

'Sure, nothing would ever happen in this country if they cancelled because of a drop of rain,' he said cheerfully. 'We'll see you soon, then, Emma.'

However, when Emma and her father arrived at the Ennis showgrounds, there was no sign of the Nolans. In fact, there weren't many people around. A few men were beginning to hammer some stakes into the ground to make the rings, and there were some children running around with a large collection of dogs.

'I just can't get used to the way nothing ever starts on time in this country,' muttered Steve. 'For good-ness' sake, Emma, try to stop Heidi lunging at every dog. Make her behave herself.'

It's all very well for you to complain, thought Emma rebelliously. You never do anything to help me. Her arm ached from Heidi's straining at the leash, and she was beginning to wish that she hadn't come. At least the rain had stopped and the sun was coming out.

'Please register immediately for the obedience class,' the loudspeaker announced. Miserably Emma went over to the tent and paid her entrance fee. There was still no sign of Orla or Mr Nolan; in fact, there was no one else in the tent. So 'immediately' probably meant 'within the next hour or so'.

Heidi was wildly excited, and Emma knew that there was little chance that she would behave the way she did when they were practising in the Big Meadow.

'I was the first one to register,' she said to her father. 'There doesn't seem to be anyone else there yet. I think I'll go and throw Heidi's bone for her over in that far corner, near the hedge, and see if I can get her to settle down a bit before the competition starts. She works much better if she's tired.'

'Hadn't you better practise your exercises?' asked Steve nervously.

'No,' said Emma. I wish Mum didn't have to work this weekend, she thought. He's making me nervous.

'See you,' she said aloud. She raced away with Heidi, deliberately exciting her so she would be less frisky when the time of the competition came.

After she and Heidi had run around for about ten minutes, Emma was immensely relieved to see the Nolans' van come bumping across the field.

'There's Orla and Tinker,' she said to Heidi. Heidi put her head on one side, listening to the familiar names; then she saw the van and went racing across the grass.

'Heidi, come back,' shouted Emma, racing after her, afraid that Heidi would get under the wheels of the van. Luckily, Mr Nolan had seen her; he slowed almost to a stop, and Emma caught up with Heidi and snapped the lead onto her collar.

'Well, aren't ye nice and early,' said Mr Nolan, unwinding himself from the van and submitting to a rapturous welcome from Heidi.

'My father is always early for everything,' said Emma, patting Tinker.

'Well, that's the English for you! Great people for being on time. Things are a bit slower around here, but they get done in the end. The English find it hard to get used to, though.'

Emma giggled. It was a good job that her father hadn't yet made his way across the field. He got very upset if anyone called him English; he always told everyone that he was as Irish as they were. They all smiled politely, but no one believed a word of it.

'I've put Heidi down for the obedience class for dogs under a year old,' she said to Orla. 'Are you going to enter Tinker?'

Orla shook her head. 'No,' she said. 'Dad says he's not ready for it yet, and he might put Heidi off. You know how they get silly together. I'll put him in for some other classes, though. Let's go across and look. Give me some money, Dad, and we'll go and have a Coke first.'

'Will we have time for that before the obedience class?' asked Emma.

'All the time in the world,' Mr Nolan assured her. 'Sure, they won't start for another hour. No one much is here yet.'

Emma began to feel better after she and Orla had had a bar of chocolate and a can of Coke each. They sat on the wall and watched all the cars and vans arrive. One van had a kennel's name on it, and when its back doors were opened a stream of German shepherds came out — noble-looking dogs, long-haired bitches, enchanting, playful pups. Emma couldn't stop looking at them.

'Come on,' said Orla, tugging at her sleeve. 'Let's go and choose the classes.'

There were plenty of people in the tent now, all chatting to one another. The two girls could hardly get near the desk, but the list of classes was pinned up on the side of the tent, so they could decide before they went to pay their money.

'Well, I'm putting Tinker in for the "dog the judge would most like to take home",' said Orla, 'and I think I'll try him in the "any variety puppy". What are you going to put Heidi in for?'

'Well, I'll try her in the "pedigree puppy",' said Emma. 'I don't think she'll win, though; there are lots of very good dogs here, and she's bound to misbehave. What else do you think I should go in for?'

'You could try the "dog who looks most like its owner",' said Orla. 'I always think that you and Heidi look quite alike. You've both got blond hair and brown eyes.'

Emma laughed, but she felt quite pleased. There was no doubt that Heidi was glamorous. Maybe, she thought, when I grow up I'll be glamorous too.

'OK, then,' she said, blushing slightly. 'Let's go and pay our money.'

The obedience class was a bit of a disaster, but Emma wasn't too upset. True, Heidi got practically no marks for walking on the lead; she pulled like a little steam engine in her efforts to catch up with the dog in front, and Emma was hot with shame as she tried to control her. When Emma had to leave Heidi sitting, walk away and then call her, Heidi decided that she wasn't going to be parted from Emma; she trotted after her immediately.

However, although she fidgeted during the two-minute stay, she did stay where Emma had left her.

So her final marks weren't too bad, and the judge was very encouraging.

'She's a lovely dog, pet,' she said kindly to Emma. 'Just a bit too fond of her own way and a bit excitable, but she'll settle down. It's good that you're training her from an early age. You'll be proud of her soon, when you get her under control.'

'Not bad, not bad at all,' said Mr Nolan, when Emma showed him the marks.

'Come on,' said Orla. 'It's time for the "dog who looks most like its owner". I've gone in for it after all. Dad said I might as well, since Tinker and I both have brown hair.'

The 'dog who looks most like its owner' competition was great fun. Eventually it was won by a big, fat, bald-headed man with a big, fat bulldog. Emma came third with Heidi.

'Now for the "pedigree puppy",' said Emma, pinning on her number.

'Are you nervous?' asked Orla.

'Not really,' said Emma. 'I think Heidi's settling down now, and at least she won't disgrace me. Anyway, I'm Number 11, and that's my lucky number.'

As soon as they entered the ring, Emma saw the judge's eye go to Heidi. He likes her, she thought, and a little thrill went through her.

'Walk your dogs,' said the judge. Everyone began to parade their dogs around. Mr Nolan had advised Emma to keep Heidi's favourite rubber bone in the top pocket of her anorak. It made a rather peculiar bulge, but as they walked around, Emma could see what a clever idea it was: Heidi kept her eyes fixed on it all the time, and the result was that, for one of the few times in her life, she walked beautifully to heel.

'Stop,' said the judge, and everyone obediently stopped. The judge looked around the ring and then muttered some numbers to his assistant.

'Numbers 8, 11, 19, 25, and 29, please stay,' the assistant announced. 'Thank you, everyone else.'

In a minute the ring was cleared, except for five people and their dogs. Emma was the only young person amongst them, and she felt very nervous when the judge told them to walk around again. She tried to concentrate on keeping Heidi's attention on her.

'Position your dogs,' said the judge.

Emma looked anxiously around to see what the other four people were doing. They seemed to be lining up their dogs to show off their best points. One man even picked up his dog by the scruff of the neck and dropped it into a perfect pose.

'Stand, Heidi,' said Emma, as firmly as she could. Heidi looks like she's going to get bored with this soon, she thought. I must get her attention.

'Where's your bone, then?' she said softly.

That did it. Heidi fixed her glowing amber-gold eyes on Emma, her tall ears alert and pricked forward. Every fibre of the young dog's body seemed to be alive with excitement and tension.

The judge beckoned to Emma. For a moment Emma thought that she had to leave the ring, but then the judge showed her where to stand and placed a man with a golden retriever behind her and a woman with a springer spaniel behind him.

It was only when the judge handed Emma the silver cup that she realised what had happened. Heidi had come first!

For the rest of the afternoon, Emma walked around in a happy daze. Even her father was thrilled and excited. He got into conversation with the woman who had the van full of German shepherds, and she petted and praised Heidi and said that when she was older Emma might think of breeding from her.

'Take her out as much as possible,' she advised Emma. 'Take her down to the town, anywhere where she'll meet other people and other dogs. The worst thing you can do is keep her at home.'

Emma smiled and nodded, and then went across to watch Tinker win first prize in the 'dog the judge would most like to take home' competition. It was a wonderful end to the day, and Orla and Emma were both wild with excitement.

'Well, I call that really great,' said Steve. 'That deserves a celebration. Let's all go and have some beefburgers before we go home. Wait until your mother sees that cup, Emma!'

CHAPTER EIGHT

All the way home from the dog show, Emma was composing a message to Bruce in her mind. First she would tell him about the obedience class and pretend she was depressed — and then she would tell him about Heidi coming first, first out of thirty puppies! She would make it really exciting. She knew that Bruce liked nice long letters; he got so bored, lying in hospital while all his gang were out surfing or going to coffee bars.

When she got home, however, there was a message waiting for her. She noticed when it had come in, and frowned with puzzlement: surely that would be the middle of the night in Australia? She sat down to read it.

```
From:      bruce.mcm@clubi.com.au
To:        emma@drumshee.ie
```

Dear Emma,

```
I'm writing to you in the middle of the
night because I can't sleep. This is a dead,
dead secret over here — it isn't something I
can tell any of my friends in Sydney — so
it's nice having a friend on the other side
of the world.

This evening my mother came to see me. There
was obviously something wrong with her. She
had loads of make-up on, but you could still
see that she'd been crying. I asked her what
was wrong. In the beginning she wouldn't tell
```

me, but eventually she started to cry again,
and then she told me the whole story.

The police have been questioning my father.
You remember I told you he's a bank manager?
Well, a big sum of money has gone missing
from an account at the bank. The account was
what they call a 'dead account' — no one had
touched the money in it for ages; it belonged
to a rich old miser. Then he died, and the
lawyers doing his will discovered that a
hundred thousand dollars had been taken out
of the account via the computer, by someone
using a password that only my father, as the
bank manager, would know.

The stupid thing is that my father hates
computers and never uses them. Believe it or
not — and the police certainly don't — he
had actually forgotten the password. It was
set two years ago, and he'd never used it
since.

The trouble is that no one else knew the
password. My father is quite sure of that.
He never told anyone, not even my mother.

I don't know what will happen now. He might
go to jail. The high-up bods in the bank
have given him a month to repay the money
and then to resign, and if he does that they
won't prosecute. The trouble is, my father
hasn't got the money; and even if he could
raise it by selling our house, my mother
says that he won't, because that would be
admitting that he did it. If you could just
know him, Emma, you'd know that he's the
last man in the world to touch a cent that
doesn't belong to him.

I hope you don't mind, but I don't feel like
playing chess tonight. I just wanted to get
that off my mind. I don't know what to do.
All I can do is lie on this bed with my mind
going around and around in circles.

Emma gasped with horror. Quickly she reread the message. Poor Bruce! What a dreadful thing to happen — almost the worst thing in the world. She sat staring at the screen and wishing she could help him. She could hear her father whistling to himself as he made tea in the kitchen, and she thought how awful it would be if anything like that happened to him. Of course, she thought, he wouldn't be like Bruce's father; Dad knows all about computers ....

As she thought that, an idea dawned on her. She printed out Bruce's message and took it into the kitchen.

'Dad,' she said. 'Let me make the tea, and you read this.'

Her father took the sheet of paper in his hand, fumbling for his reading-glasses, and sat down at the kitchen table to read it through. Emma busied herself with the kettle and the mugs. Neither of them said anything for a long time. Emma could see by her father's face that he was thinking hard, turning over various possibilities.

She placed the mugs of tea and the biscuit tin on the table and sat down beside him. Steve sipped his tea absent-mindedly. Then he took off his reading-glasses and laid them on the table, turning the piece of paper over in his hands.

'Now, Emma,' he said, 'there are two ways of looking at this. The first, and the simplest, is that the bank is right: Bruce's father stole the money from the account. Yes, I know, I know, Bruce says that's impossible; but then, every man's own family believes in him. It would be a sad world if they didn't.'

'But Bruce said that his father didn't even remember

his password. That proves he couldn't have used it to steal the money.'

'Sounds very suspicious to me,' said her father, in the shocked tones of one to whom computers were as familiar as cups of tea. 'Still, let's look at the less likely, but more interesting — to me, anyway — possibility: that he didn't do it, but someone else did, using his password.'

'Yes, but,' Emma began, 'Bruce said no one else knew his password.'

'Depends on the password he chose,' said Steve. 'Now, if I asked you to choose a password for your computer, what would you choose?'

Emma thought for a minute. 'I think I'd choose "Heidi",' she said.

'There you are,' said her father triumphantly. 'A lot of people choose the names of past or present pets for their passwords. So if I was a hacker, trying to get at all those millions which you have salted away in a secret electronic bank account, I'd just have to hang around the lanes here for an hour or two and hear you shouting "Heidi", and then I'd try that out as a password.'

'And if that didn't work?'

'Well, there's a list of other very common passwords: owner's second name, second name backwards, wife's second name, mother's maiden name, date of birth backwards, favourite composer .... Anyway, what time is it?'

'Six o'clock. Why?'

'Well, your young man may possibly be still awake. It should be about five o'clock in the morning in Sydney. Let's go send him a message.'

Emma sat at her computer while her father dictated.

```
From:        emma@drumshee.ie
To:          bruce.mcm@clubi.com.au

Is it possible to let my father know your
father's password? He says that he can tell
if it's one of the most common ones, which
would mean that someone else could have worked
it out. I know it's probably a secret, but my
father makes most of his living by working
on security measures for computer software,
and he just might be able to help you.
```

Bruce must have been awake: when Emma checked her mail, only half an hour later, his answer was there.

```
From:        bruce.mcm@clubi.com.au
To:          emma@drumshee.ie

It's no secret now. The password has been
cancelled. It's a nonsense word, that's why
my father couldn't remember it. He was warned
never to write it down, so he tried to memo-
rise it, but of course he forgot it. Knowing
him, I think he didn't want to admit that
he'd forgotten it, so he just kept away from
the account. Anyway, the word — if you can
call it a word — is 'cambidur'. It has no
meaning, no relevance to anything.
```

Steve stared at the word for a few minutes, trying it under his breath, spelling it backwards. Then he seized Emma's homework jotter and tried splitting the word up and reassembling it. Finally he shook his head.

'No,' he said. 'If it's true that he didn't write it down, then no hacker could have guessed this one. Let me write the boy a message.'

Pushing Emma aside, he typed:

```
From:        steve@drumshee.ie
To:          bruce.mcm@clubi.com.au

Bruce, I'm Emma's father and I'll work on your
problem. I'll give Emma a list of questions
for you; you'll find them waiting for you at
about eight o'clock tomorrow morning, your
time. You'll have to ask your father to co-
operate with me. Tell him that I've probably
cracked harder problems than this one.

Don't worry. Keep your chin up and go to
sleep now.
```

Emma stared at her father hopefully. 'Do you really think you can crack it?'

'Why not? I'm sure I've cracked worse ones. I'll work on it now, if you'll get the dinner ready. Your mother will be home in about an hour.'

'Not only will I get the dinner,' said Emma solemnly, 'but if you solve this for poor old Bruce and his father, then I'll never argue with you again.'

'Hey,' said her father good-humouredly, 'let's not make promises we can't keep. I'll do my best — that's all any of us can do.'

As Emma scrubbed the potatoes, she could hear him humming to himself in the study. She smiled. He's happy that we're friends, she thought. I suppose I must have been a bit of a pain during the last few months.

She set the table and placed the beautiful silver cup on the top shelf of the dresser, just above the shelf where her own cups from chess tournaments were kept.

'Now you look at that,' she said to Heidi. 'You got

that cup because, for once, you were behaving yourself. Keep it up and you might fill that top shelf with
them. I bet it'll be the first thing Mum sees when she
comes in.'

Joyce was tired when she came in, but not so tired
that she failed to notice Emma and Heidi, one on
either side of the dresser, both looking up at the
magnificent silver cup. She stopped in the doorway.

'Am I seeing things?' she asked. 'Don't tell me she
won that!'

Emma had only just finished telling her mother all
about the dog show, and all about Bruce's problem,
when Steve burst out of his study, his reading-glasses
pushed crookedly down on his nose.

'I think I might have got it,' he said excitedly. 'It's
pretty simple really, but they may have overlooked
it. You see, Emma, all big computer systems have a
special way of keeping track of the users. Every time
someone uses a password, the computer records the
time and date on an optical disk. This can't be tampered
with, so it should be possible to get the date and time
when the password was used to open this account.
Then, with a bit of luck, Bruce's father will have an
alibi. It's very unlikely that the fraud would have
been committed during office hours.'

'Oh, that's brilliant!' cried Emma, hugging her
father.

'I wish I had a clue what you two are talking
about when you get on to computers,' said Joyce.

'You just go and change, Mum, and I'll e-mail
Bruce, and then we'll all eat,' said Emma happily.

'No, leave it until later,' said her father. 'Let the
lad have a few hours' sleep and get his message at

the time that I told him. Let's hope it works. And, Emma, go on with the chess game; it will take his mind off things. I was having a look at your game. He's a very good player. You should have some great games, the two of you.'

CHAPTER NINE

Sunday had been a good day, all in all. There had been Heidi's great success; and although Emma was sorry for Bruce, she had faith in her father's ability to sort the matter out. But Monday — well, Monday was a terrible day.

For a start, Heidi was a real pain in the morning. When Emma took her out, she suddenly darted away to the edge of the field, put her front paws on the wall and started to bark angrily at a farmer who was building a haystack in the corner of the next field. Emma screamed at her and ran to grab her by the collar before she actually climbed over the wall. The farmer was so frightened that he had climbed to the top of the haystack, and when Emma apologised, he said nothing — just stood there, with the pitchfork in his hand, looking very annoyed. Emma hoped desperately that he wouldn't tell her father and start up all the trouble about Heidi again.

She was too worried to eat her breakfast. As soon as she could, she escaped into her bedroom, switched on her computer and checked her e-mail. Nothing from Bruce, not even a chess move. In a bad mood, Emma set off for school, only to find that Orla was not there.

'She and my dad are both sick in bed,' said Orla's younger sister Carol. 'My dad said to tell you that he won't be up for Heidi's lesson today.'

Both of them sick! Emma thought guiltily about

the beefburgers they had eaten after the dog show. Perhaps there had been something wrong with them. She didn't feel all that great herself; but, of course, she and her father lived on beefburgers, so they were probably immune to whatever was put into them.

With a scowl, she sat down at her desk and opened her book. It was a book that her father had given her; it was about a computer language called Java. Emma was finding it very difficult, and she was only too glad to put it down when the girl whose name she couldn't pronounce came up to her and asked to look at it.

'You wouldn't understand it,' said Emma, without thinking. 'It's a computer language.'

'You think you're so clever, don't you?' sneered the girl. 'You're just stuck-up. My dad says that English people shouldn't be allowed to buy houses here in Ireland. You should stay in your own country.'

'Mind your own business,' snapped Emma. 'And tell your dad to mind his own business too.'

'And you've got a really wicked dog. It even went for the priest. You should shoot it, my dad says.'

White with anger, Emma picked up the book on Java and flung it straight into the girl's sneering face.

'There you are, then! You said you wanted to read it!' she shouted.

'What on earth is going on here?' said the teacher, opening the door and walking in on the scene of chaos.

By lunch-time, Emma was miserable. No one seemed to be speaking to her; the teacher had been shocked at her behaviour; Heidi was still as badly behaved as ever; and Bruce was in real trouble.

Chapter Nine

Emma had had enough. She picked up her bag and walked defiantly out of the school.

She had gone about a hundred yards when she began to realise how stupid she was being. Today would pass, and Orla would be back tomorrow. And as for Heidi, it was silly to expect her to turn into a well-trained dog overnight; she would just have to keep training her.

At the thought of Heidi's golden face, Emma began to feel a bit better. She turned around and slowly went back to the school.

A group of girls were standing at the gate. I'll kill them if they say anything, Emma thought; but no one said a word. She marched past them, went back into the classroom and took up her battered copy of *Java Programming for the Beginner*. She didn't care if they thought she was showing off; at least it would hide her face until lessons began again.

As soon as she got home, Emma checked her e-mail again, but there was still no message from Bruce. I'll mail him this evening, she thought, whether or not I hear from him.

'Come on, Heidi, let's go up to the Cathaireen Field,' she said.

They climbed up the steep path and went through the *cathair* into the Cathaireen Field. Emma threw the rubber bone for Heidi until they were both puffed out; then she put the bone to one side and practised sits, stays and recalls. Heidi wasn't too bad at the sits and the stays — at least, if there was nothing to dis- tract her — but she was very bad at coming when she was called. Emma practised the recall again and again, but Heidi just sauntered across the field as if

69

she were doing Emma a favour by indulging her in this boring new game. Emma began to get more and more annoyed with her.

Then an idea struck her. She picked up Heidi's bone and walked across the field, waving the pink rubber bone and shouting, 'Sit, Heidi, sit.'

When she turned around, Heidi was still sitting, but she was no longer looking bored. Her mouth was open, her tongue was hanging out, her ears were as erect as they could possibly be and her eyes were fixed intently on the bone.

'Come, Heidi, come,' shouted Emma, and Heidi shot across the field like an arrow released from a bow.

'Well,' said Emma, rubbing the soft fur behind Heidi's ears, 'if you'd only do that at a show, you might win another cup. Let's try that again.'

Emma tried the same trick again, and again Heidi pelted across the field and skidded to a halt just in front of Emma, looking like the best-trained dog in the world. Elated by her success, Emma threw the bone up in the air, as high as she could, and Heidi rushed around like a lunatic, giving short, excited barks.

'Let's go in and tell Dad how clever you are,' said Emma eventually, when they were both exhausted.

Steve, however, was in no mood to discuss Heidi's cleverness. Behind his terrible old black-framed spectacles, his eyes were gleaming with excitement as he peered at the screen of his computer.

'Had a good day at school?' he asked, his fingers never ceasing their pattering on the keyboard.

'Yeah,' said Emma.

'Good,' Steve replied.

Bet he'd say that if I told him I burned down the school and murdered one or two girls today, thought Emma, as she went into the kitchen. She fed Heidi, made herself a cup of tea and took out a couple of biscuits. She switched on the TV, and, picking up the remote control, sat down on the couch.

Heidi jumped up beside her and put her head on Emma's lap. Heidi wasn't really allowed on chairs, but the furniture in the kitchen was old stuff, and Emma was feeling a bit lonely. She kissed the top of Heidi's warm, furry head and flicked from channel to channel, trying to find something interesting to watch. Really, she thought with irritation, Sky is almost as bad as RTÉ. She wished they had BBC, but there was some mountain or other in the way.

In the end, in desperation, she went over to the Family Channel. It'll probably be something stupid about gardening or decorating, she thought; but by some miracle, it was showing a documentary about mountain-rescue dogs.

'Just look at that, Heidi!' Emma said, the end of her biscuit falling soggily into her tea as she watched the handsome German shepherd jump eagerly into a helicopter.

'This dog is so good at tracking that helicopters arrive for him from all over Europe,' said the voice of the narrator. 'He's not afraid of the helicopters, then?' he asked the dog's owner, thrusting the microphone under the man's nose.

'Not a bit,' said the man easily, with a strong Irish accent. 'He's mad on helicopters. Whenever he sees one up in the sky, he starts whining with excitement. He thinks it must be coming for him.'

'That's an Irish dog, Heidi,' said Emma.

Heidi put a paw on her knee and whined slightly.

'Yes, I know, it's not fair,' said Emma. 'Never mind, when you're completely trained then you'll have helicopters coming for you, too. Now, watch, Heidi. See, they're putting the harness on the dog — and look at him zooming up the mountain! Oh, Heidi, you'd love doing that!'

Emma was so excited that she didn't even notice Heidi eating her second biscuit. The dog on the TV zigzagged up the mountain, nose almost glued to the ground, until, beside a large clump of heather, he stopped and began to dig frantically in some soft soil.

'Good boy, good boy,' encouraged his breathless trainer. 'What have you found, then?'

What the dog had found was some buried clothing. The trainer took it out of the hole in the ground, gave the excited dog a warm hug and a few pats, and then turned to face the cameras again.

'This is a training exercise,' he explained. 'Most of our work is done in the Kerry mountains, or the Welsh mountains, or even in Switzerland; and in the winter, it often means digging people out of the snow.'

'He seems to enjoy his work, anyway,' commented the interviewer.

'He certainly does that. You notice I praised him when he found the clothes — now, most police dogs get fed chocolate when they make a find, but I don't need to do that. This dog works for the sake of working. He's like those people over in the stock market in London; he's what you call a workaholic.'

Emma giggled to herself. She got the biscuit tin and placed it on the couch beside her. She took a biscuit for herself and handed another one to Heidi.

'And what made you go in for this sort of thing?' enquired the interviewer.

'Well, it was like this. I had this dog, and I've never known such a terrible dog as he was. You had to spend hours playing with him or taking him for walks, or else he got into mischief. He had a rubber ball that he was mad about, and when my arm was tired from throwing it, I used to hide it and give myself a few minutes' peace while he was hunting for it. And do you know, even as a puppy he'd never give up until he found it. He wouldn't even go for his dinner until he found that ball.'

Emma jumped up from the couch, switched off the television and firmly put the lid back on the biscuit tin.

'No more,' she said sternly. 'We're both going to get fat. Come on. Let's see if you're as clever as that dog on the TV. Where's that bone of yours?'

Heidi seemed to catch Emma's mood of excitement. They both raced up the steep path towards the *cathair*. One side of the fort had been roughly dug up by Steve. At Easter, when they had just arrived, he had planned to have a vegetable garden there; but the heavy clay and the thick roots of rushes had defeated him, and now there was just a pile of over-turned sods and a rusting spade left sticking in the ground. That would be a good place to bury the bone, thought Emma, as she led Heidi into the Cathaireen Field and tied her to a blackthorn bush.

Heidi yelped with excitement when she saw Emma going off with the bright pink bone, and she kept up a tremendous racket all the time that Emma

73

was covering the bone with a few clods of earth. As soon as Emma released her, she shot away, through the gap and into the fort, her nose to the ground, just like the dog on TV.

Emma could hardly believe it when Heidi stopped and began to dig with her strong little paws. In a moment, the muddy bone was exposed, and Heidi pranced around happily with the bone sticking out of her mouth like a giant pink cigar.

'That was too easy for you, Heidi,' said Emma, her voice trembling with excitement. 'I'll have to bury it a bit deeper next time.'

She led Heidi back into the Cathaireen Field and tied her up again. This time Heidi made an even greater racket. It's a good job we're about a mile from the nearest house, thought Emma. She wasn't worried about her father coming out; when he was programming, he was blind and deaf to the world around him.

This time she went into the centre of the fort and began to dig a little hole, right in the middle of a clump of marsh irises. It was hard work, and Emma could see why her father had abandoned the vegetable garden.

When she had buried the bone, she went back to fetch Heidi.

CHAPTER TEN

From: emma@drumshee.ie
To: bruce.mcm@clubi.com.au

Dear Bruce,

I hope everything is working out for your father. Please let us know. My father will have some other ideas if that one doesn't work out, but please get in touch anyway. I'd love to hear from you, and that's a cool game of chess we're playing. I was going through it last night and thinking how good it was.

Anyway, wait till you hear about Heidi's latest. I saw a film on TV about a man who trained his dog to find people who are lost on mountains, and then I thought I'd train Heidi to find her bone if I buried it. So I took her out to the old fort — you remember that old Iron Age fort? The *cathair* that your great-great-grandfather had marked on the map? Well, she found the bone, but also, her digging uncovered the entrance to a secret underground room! Dad has got the builders coming to make the entrance safe so we can go down. I'm so excited! Maybe we'll find buried treasure!

Love,

Emma

Emma stopped typing and looked up towards the fort. It was such a lovely day that she had taken her laptop outside; she was sitting on the stone wall near the entrance to the fort.

She let her mind drift. She almost didn't want the builders to come, in case they found out that there was nothing in the underground room after all. At the moment, she could imagine so many wonderful things — gold, silver ....

She smiled to herself. 'More likely spiders, Heidi,' she said aloud. She carried the laptop inside and sent off her message.

```
From:       bruce.mcm@clubi.com.au
To:         emma@drumshee.ie
```

Dear Emma,

That was a really good idea your father came up with, and it gave us all a bit of hope. The police did as you suggested — and, to give them their due, they did it all very quickly.

They found out that the money was withdrawn from the account, using my father's user- name, which apparently has priority access, at eight o'clock in the evening. My father always leaves the bank before six, so it looked as if we'd proved it couldn't have been him; but, unfortunately, my mother was up visiting me in hospital that day, and there are no witnesses to prove that he didn't go back into the bank.

My mother said it was all very unfortunate, because when the police questioned my father, he said that he'd been watching TV all that evening. Naturally they asked him what had been on the TV, and he said he'd been watching the cricket. The cricket was the advertised programme, and I'm sure my father meant to watch it, but he did what he always does — fell asleep almost as soon as he'd turned on the TV, and only woke up in time for the nine o'clock news. What he didn't know was that the cricket match had been cancelled due to an electric storm. So, as he didn't want to tell the police that he'd been asleep, he told them that he'd seen the cricket match, and now they think he was just lying. In any case, they keep coming back, very politely, to the fact that not only was his username used, but so was his password.

Will you ask your father if he can think of any other possibilities, please? It's all getting very desperate. My mother's in a terrible state and my father just looks frozen.

That's very interesting about the underground room. While I've been lying here, I accessed a website that's all about the first millennium, and it had quite a bit about Iron Age forts. And guess what? They usually had an underground room, called a souterrain. When my father came to see me, I told him all about your discovery; and you'll never believe this, but apparently the word 'souterrain' is written in the middle of the Cathaireen Field in the map that my great-great-grandfather drew. My father says he often wondered whether there were any remains of it left.

I wouldn't be too hopeful about finding treasure, though. The McMahons were pretty poor, and if they had any treasure I'd say it would have been sold at some stage.

Still, it should be very interesting. I wish I could see it.

My next chess move is:

13   d4 - f5

How do you like that, eh?

From: emma@drumshee.ie
To: bruce.mcm@clubi.com.au

13   e7 - f6

Now what are you going to do with your poor
little queen?

I've been talking to my father and he says
that now that the exact time is known, the
police should check the alibi of whoever is
Sysman, which means Systems Manager. (He says
some people call it Sysadmin, but I like
Sysman better. It sounds like something out
of Star Trek, doesn't it?) Anyway, apparently
Sysman has access to almost every part of the
program — except, unfortunately, the passwords.
But my dad says it's worth a try, because
Sysmen have been known to boldly go to places
where in theory they shouldn't be going.

We haven't had the souterrain (you're right,
that's what my father thinks it is) checked
yet, and I'm not allowed to go near it until
the builders come. The roof of it is made
from flagstones, just like the roof of the
old cottage here, and my father is afraid it
might cave in.

I had a look at that website about the first
millennium, too. It's really weird to think
that we're going into the third millennium,
and yet there might be parts of Drumshee
that haven't changed all that much since the
first one.

By the way, one day when Mr Nolan was here, he
showed me a strange little place underneath
an old ash tree, all blocked in with blackthorn bushes — a stone shrine with a little
stone figure in it. He said it was a shrine to
Saint Brigid, but my father thinks the statue
is actually some sort of Celtic earth goddess.
Another link with the first millennium!

I do wish you could come over. After all,

we're practically cousins. Maybe when your leg is better you might be allowed. It would be nice to have a bit of company. My father has a big new job on, and he's like a zombie most of the time; and my mother's working all hours of the day, and sometimes of the night, at Ennis Hospital. It's a good job I have Heidi. She's great company. Mr Nolan and Orla are both well again, so we're going on with the lessons.

Next Saturday we're all going into Ennis to walk Heidi around. If you hear on the international news that Ennis has been cleared by a savage guard dog, you'll know how it turned out. I'm a bit nervous. I hate people disliking Heidi. She's so gorgeous with me that I want everyone else to love her like I do.

Anyway, she's getting on really well with tracking. Mr Nolan is quite impressed; he says I'll have to try her in field trials when she's a bit more settled. She certainly has the makings of a tracker dog, he says.

🖳

From: bruce.mcm@clubi.com.au
To: emma@drumshee.ie

Dear Emma,

My queen is perfectly happy with your last move, thank you very much. Our reply is:

14   c3 - g3!

I'm afraid your father will have to do a bit more thinking. The police did look at the alibi for the Sysman (yes, there is one), but it turned out he was surfing at the time, with twenty other people, so that's no go.

Let me know as soon as you explore the souterrain. I was talking to my dad about it last night, just to try to distract him, and he got quite interested. He says he seems to remember hearing, when he was quite young, about something very valuable being found there once. He can't remember the details, but he says he'd love to hear more.

I told him that you invited me over, but that was the wrong thing to say. Immediately he thought about money, and then he thought about this wretched business, and he just got up and left. I'm sure my mother was sorry to see him home again so soon. He's been suspended from the bank, 'pending investigations', and he doesn't know what to do with himself all day.

⌨

From: emma@drumshee.ie
To: bruce.mcm@clubi.com.au

Dear Bruce,

Your queen move wasn't a great surprise. I think the most sensible thing for me to do is:

14   d7 - e5

It's time I took the war down to your end of the board for a change. You're getting your own way a bit too much for my liking!

What a shame that the Sysman had an alibi. Any chance of him slipping away by submarine and doing a quick burglary?

My father says to tell you not to worry too much. He has an idea in the back of his mind about how the account could have been robbed, but he doesn't want to say anything until he can check out all the bits and pieces. You see, he has a very big job on at the moment, and he's spending most of his time on-line to Dublin. He's setting up a secure database for a firm there. He says he should be finished in a day or two, and then he'll be able to put his mind to your problem.

I'm sorry I have no better news for you, but I thought I'd better write anyway. At least it'll give you something to do: think out your next chess move!

The builders still haven't come, so no news on the souterrain. What a shame that the treasure has already been found! I wonder what it was.

💻

From: bruce.mcm@clubi.com.au
To: emma@drumshee.ie

Dear Emma,

OK, then. Let's do battle. My answer is — wait for it —

15   c1 - f4

No news from here. I am thoroughly fed up. What's Heidi doing these days?

💻

From: emma@drumshee.ie
To: bruce.mcm@clubi.com.au

Dear Bruce,

Two can play at your little game. Don't imagine that I can't see what you're up to.

15   d8 - c7

As for Heidi, she was absolutely atrocious when we took her into Ennis. She was wildly excited; I think she thought she was going to another dog show. Unfortunately, Dad and Mum and I arrived early — well, on time, really, but that *is* early here. I kept telling Dad to leave it a bit later, but he always has to leave himself extra time in case of problems, so when we got to the car park there was no sign of Orla and her dad.

As soon as we took Heidi out of the car, she shot across the road towards the river — she almost pulled my arm off. There were some people there, feeding swans, and they nearly died of heart failure when Heidi came storming up, barking her head off. I just couldn't keep her back. Anyway, Dad nearly had a fit and went around apologising to everyone, and Mum tried to convince him that Heidi was only barking at the swans. (I don't know why it's better to bark at swans than to bark at stupid people, but Mum is always trying to keep the peace between Dad and me.)

By the time the Nolans arrived, Dad was having a real fit of nerves and wanted to take Heidi home again. But good old Mr Nolan calmed him down and said the dog would just have to get used to people. So eventually Dad went off to MacCool's Internet Café (his favourite place in Ennis) and Mr Nolan took Heidi for a while, and she calmed down a lot. But once she was back with me, she started lunging at dogs and even tried to take off after a jogger. Luckily Mr Nolan grabbed the lead, so between us we managed to hold her.

Then Mr Nolan got an inspiration and we went into a pet shop and bought something called a Halti. It's a bit like a horse's head-collar, and it's absolutely marvellous. I can hold Heidi as easily as anything with it, and it's given me the confidence to stand up to her and not show how panicky I am.

I'll write again tomorrow. Dad has finished that job, and now he's sitting in his study surrounded by books on security systems. Sleep well, or have a good day, depending on when this message reaches you. I always get muddled about the time differences.

CHAPTER ELEVEN

All that evening, Emma hovered around her father's study. She brought him innumerable cups of tea and sandwiches of digestive biscuits with raspberry jam in the middle.

Steve was obviously putting his whole mind to Mr McMahon's problem, and he hardly acknowledged her presence as he gulped down the tea or munched the biscuits. Emma wished she could ask him how he was getting on, but she knew that he hated his train of thought to be broken.

She peeped into her parents' bedroom, but her mother was stretched out on the bed, fast asleep, so Emma couldn't talk to her either.

She attached the lead to Heidi's collar and took her outside. Ever since that awful day in Ennis, she had been practising walking Heidi up and down the avenue. Her mother had measured the avenue on the car speedometer, and Emma had worked out that if she walked to the gate and back five times she would have walked a mile.

Heidi trotted along beside her, as good as gold. 'It's no good you trying to fool me,' said Emma fondly, looking down at the golden head. 'You'd be as great a nuisance as ever if there was anyone around.'

Mr Nolan had told Emma that good behaviour in a dog is a matter of habit, and Emma had promised to walk Heidi every single day. Perhaps it might do some good, but Emma was dubious. The big problem with Heidi was that she got bored very easily, and there was nothing to excite her while she was plodding up and down the avenue. In fact, if ever a dog expressed boredom, every line in Heidi's body was showing it now. Her big, expressive eyes were fixed on Emma, seeming to say, 'For heaven's sake, let's have a bit of fun!'

Emma bent down and stroked the shining coat. 'Never mind, Heidi,' she said aloud. 'When we've done our mile, we'll have a quick game with your bone.'

After Emma had hung up the lead and given Heidi a game, she peeped in at her mother again. Joyce was still asleep. I wish she didn't go out to work, thought Emma. She's always so tired. I'm sure she's working too hard.

She wondered what to do. It was no good writing to Bruce; she would have to wait until her father had come up with some sort of idea.

She went towards the kitchen, and as she put her hand on the doorknob she heard the kettle beginning to sing. That's a good sign, she thought. He wouldn't have got up to make more tea unless he'd discovered something.

She turned the handle of the low, old-fashioned door and went in. Her father was whistling to himself. Another good sign.

'Well, I think I might have cracked it,' he said when he saw Emma. 'It's quite simple, really; I don't know why I didn't think of it before. Now go easy, go easy,' he added, holding up a warning hand as he saw the excitement in her eyes. 'Remember what I said to you on the first day. The most likely thing is

that Bruce's father did take the money. He probably meant to put it back, but his client's death took him unawares.'

'Oh, Dad,' said Emma impatiently. She never could stand people saying the same thing over and over again.

'OK, OK, warning over,' said her father hastily. He poured the boiling water into his mug, squeezed the tea bag against the side of the mug and flipped it into the bin. 'Want a cup?'

Emma shook her head.

'Well, come into my study, then. I'll explain it to you, and you can put it into simple terms for Bruce and his father, so there will be no chance of them misunderstanding. It's no good me sending them a lot of jargon which they won't understand. You write it in your own words, and then I'll check it through for accuracy.'

It didn't take Emma long to understand her father's new theory. Over the years she had picked up a lot of computer expertise by listening to bits of conversations between her father and his friends. She made him go over it twice, to make sure she understood, and then she got up.

At the door she stopped.

'Thanks for doing all this,' she said awkwardly. 'I'm really grateful. Good job I've got a genius for a father.'

She closed the door quickly, before Steve could say anything embarrassing, but she was glad she had made herself say it. He looked really pleased.

In her bedroom she quickly logged on and sent her message.

Chapter Eleven

From: emma@drumshee.ie
To: bruce.mcm@clubi.com.au

Dear Bruce,

My father thinks he's got it!! He says to ask your father, or the police, to investigate all the staff at the bank, especially the ones with a computer background. See if there's anyone who worked for the company that installed the computer in the bank, or for the company that wrote the software for the bank computer system. If there is anyone who did — now comes the complicated bit, and they'll need a computer expert to verify this — someone will have to go through the program and see whether a 'back door' has been left in the system to allow the programmer to get back in later.

My father says that if there's a problem about doing this in Sydney, he'll be very pleased to help. His e-mail address is steve@drumshee.ie. However — and I'm quoting him — any decent programmer should be able to find this out. Tell the police they should look for something strange inside the main program, something you wouldn't expect.

I hope this all makes sense. It seems to make sense to me. It's really exciting, almost like an up-to-date detective story. By the time I'm grown-up, that might be a real profession — computer detective. Do you have Ruth Rendell stories on TV over there? You know, the ones with Inspector Wexford? I like the idea of being a computer-fraud expert and having Scotland Yard call me in whenever there's anything too complicated for poor old Inspector Wexford to solve.

By the way, the builders are coming tomorrow, so we'll find out the secrets of the souterrain quite soon. I'll keep you posted.

How's your leg these days? Do you have to

study while you're in hospital, or can you
just lie around doing what you like all the
time? You certainly have more time than I
have for thinking about chess moves. Between
school and teaching Heidi, I never seem to
have a moment.

Emma let her fingers rest on the keyboard for a
moment and stared thoughtfully at her chessboard,
which was set up on the table beside her desk. She
had a suspicion that Bruce was a better player than
she was. So far, the game seemed to be going his
way, and all her bright ideas were being forestalled.
That combination of bishop and queen on the same
line looked rather formidable.

She thought for a while, moving the pieces on the
board and wondering what to do next. Finally she
shrugged her shoulders.

'Well, Heidi, we'll just have to wait and see what
he comes up with,' she said as she sent the message.

CHAPTER TWELVE

From: bruce.mcm@clubi.com.au
To: emma@drumshee.ie

Dear Emma,

That's a really great idea your father had.
It does make sense to me, and I've asked my
mother to get one of the policemen to come
up to the hospital and see me. She wanted to
give the printout of your message to my dad,
but I persuaded her not to. Dad seems to
have given up completely. My mother says
he's so ashamed of having told the police he
watched that stupid cricket match that now
he won't do anything for himself. He lets
her do all the talking to the lawyer. I feel
awfully useless, just lying here.

Anyway, the policeman in charge isn't exactly
pushing himself — he sent a message to say
he might come in tomorrow. If I don't see
him by about tea-time, I think I'll ring him
up and at least try to talk to him.

My next move is:

16   a1 - d1 (Yeah, stodgy, I know, but basi-
cally sound.)

From: emma@drumshee.ie
To: bruce.mcm@clubi.com.au

Dear Bruce,

They say imitation is the sincerest form of
flattery, so I'll flatter you by saying:

a8 - d8

I hope you see your policeman soon, and that things get sorted out.

Orla and I and two or three of the other kids have a great idea for the summer holidays. We're going to join a surfing club down at Lahinch beach! Dad is all for the idea. I think he was afraid I'd spend the summer holidays moping around the house. He's promised to buy me my own wet suit and my own surfboard. It's a bit embarrassing, actually, because the others will be just hiring theirs. I know I'm a bit spoilt, really. I have much more pocket money than any of the others, and more things of my own — a stereo, a TV, a laptop, things like that. But Dad's afraid I might pick up germs if I wore someone else's wet suit — I don't know what germs, but he's got a thing about germs. He's always swallowing bottles of vitamin pills and sucking throat sweets.

Anyway, I'm really looking forward to learning how to surf. You must tell me a bit more about it. If you come over here when your leg is better, we can go surfing together. Orla's dad says that Lahinch is one of the best beaches in Europe for surfing. I don't know whether that's true or not; Clare people always think that everything in County Clare is the best in the world!

Keep me posted!

From: bruce.mcm@clubi.com.au
To: emma@drumshee.ie

Dear Emma,

No news yet.

17   d1 x d6

Emma stared at the message with annoyance.

'He could have written a bit more, Heidi,' she grumbled, rubbing the soft fur under the dog's ears.

She looked back through her chess notebook. Of course, she thought, I should have moved the other rook to d8. That was pretty stupid. Still, I didn't expect that last move. Bruce is certainly a good player.

She spent some time thinking out her next move, wrote it into her chess notebook, and then checked it through once again.

```
From:        emma@drumshee.ie
To:          bruce.mcm@clubi.com.au

Dear Bruce,

17                          d8 x d6
```

Sorry to hear there's no news yet. Still, keep on hoping.

The builders have arrived at last! They're propping up the roof of the entrance — it looks like a flight of stone steps going down to some sort of underground room.

They're making a big fuss about how dangerous it is and how careful they have to be; but when Heidi heard them in the fort, she went flying up there, barking her head off — with me puffing and panting behind — and guess what? Every one of the builders disappeared into that 'terribly dangerous' place! It was really funny — they all crowded in and held a big piece of wood in front of them, and one of them kept saying, 'Well, Lord tonight, that's a very wicked dog you have there.'

Anyway, I finally managed to get Heidi to come away. I locked her up in the kitchen, and then I went back and told the builders

that I hadn't known they were there and that
Heidi had thought they were burglars. They
were all OK then, so I got up my courage and
asked them not to tell my father about it or
I'd get into trouble. They all promised —
they were very nice. I asked them how long
it would be before the place was safe, and
they were a bit vague. I'll let you know
when I have some more news.

Good luck,

Emma

From: bruce.mcm@clubi.com.au
To: emma@drumshee.ie

Dear Emma,

18   f4 x e5

Best wishes,

Bruce

'Any news from the lad?' asked Steve, coming into
Emma's room as she stood staring at her computer
screen.

'Not really,' said Emma, irritated. 'Oh, he's sending me his chess moves — but other than that, not a
word. And I go to all the trouble of writing him long
letters and telling him every piece of news I can think
of. And think of all the time he has, compared to me!
He doesn't even have to go to school. He's just lying
in bed, dossing. He could write pages if he wanted to.'

'Well, maybe he's a bit depressed. Don't worry
about it. Anyway, I'd better get back to work. Let me
know if you hear anything.'

When her father had gone, Emma sat with her fingers resting irresolutely on the keyboard. She didn't really know what to say. It was like having a conversation with yourself.

That's the trouble with boys, she thought: they never talk about their worries. She remembered Darren, one of her best friends in London. His parents had got divorced, and he would never say a word about it to anyone. Emma wouldn't even have known he was so upset if it hadn't been for the fact that he had started playing really pathetic chess. She had longed to comfort him, but she hadn't been able to think of anything to say.

At least it's easier in a virtual relationship than in a face-to-face one, she thought. You don't have to worry about blushing or looking stupid.

However, there was no point in going on trying to be jolly and pretending that everything was all right for Bruce. When Emma thought of what she would feel if her father were in that sort of trouble, she almost felt sick.

She took a deep breath and began to type.

```
From:      emma@drumshee.ie
To:        bruce.mcm@clubi.com.au

Dear Bruce,

I keep trying to imagine what it must be
like for you. It must make it so much worse
that you can't do anything but think. If you
could go to school, it would take your mind
off things for a bit.

Please don't think I'm being bossy or any-
thing, but I think it would be good for you
to have an assignment — something you really
```

```
*have* to do. So here goes. If you don't do
this within a few days, I'm not going to
speak to you any more.
```

'Well, I never do speak to him anyway,' Emma explained to Heidi. 'I just write to him, and I can always go on writing to him if this doesn't work.'

She thought for a moment and then continued her rapid typing, the little clicking sounds filling the peaceful room.

```
I'd really love to know more about Sydney.
All the girls at school watch *Neighbours*,
and they're always asking me questions and I
never know the answers. So please write and
tell me everything you can think of about
Sydney — the names of the places, what the
weather is like, what sort of shops there
are. Has it just got one beach, or are there
lots? What class are you in at school, and
what do you study? Do you have homework, or
do you call it something different, like
'prep'? Have you ever been to the famous
Opera House?

I'd love to see Sydney. Dad says he might
arrange for our family to go there for a
holiday.
```

Emma paused again. She didn't want to remind Bruce of his father's money troubles; but, on the other hand, she didn't want him to think that the whole of her family was going to land in his house.

```
We'd be staying in a hotel, but you and I
would be able to meet. Don't send me a photo-
graph, and I won't send one to you either.
Then it'll be a surprise when we meet each
other. Anyway, I always look terrible in
photos. I think I look like a horse.
```

Emma stopped typing. She went over to the mirror and studied herself. She wished her hair didn't hang down so straight on either side of her face. She had to have a fringe, or her hair would be in her eyes all the time, but she hated her fringe; she thought it looked really old-fashioned, really sad. Her eyes were OK, she decided; they were a nice golden-brown. But her face was too pale.

She sighed, and Heidi nosed her leg and sighed deeply also.

'Well, what are you complaining about?' asked Emma, looking down at the dog fondly. 'I suppose you think we should be going out. It can't be your face that you're worrying about. As for your hair — well, I've never known you to have a bad hair day. And your eyes are gorgeous, and you have the cutest black pencilling around them. I wish I was allowed to wear eyeliner like you do, Heidi!'

Heidi put her head on one side, trying to understand the unfamiliar words, and Emma had to laugh at herself.

'I must be going around the twist, talking to the dog all day long,' she muttered. 'Well, I suppose it's easier than trying to write letters to someone who just says "e7" in return.'

She went back to her desk and sat down in front of her keyboard again.

```
By the way, the builders have got most of
the roof over the steps to the underground
room shored up, so I'll be able to go in
soon. I bet there's nothing there, though.
I'm sure the builders have been in and out
of it (and not just when Heidi has them
afraid for their lives, either!). I went up
```

to the fort the other day, at lunch-time, and there was no sign of them, but I could hear their voices. I think they were eating their sandwiches down there!

18   d6 - d1

Best wishes,

Emma

From: bruce.mcm@clubi.com.au
To: emma@drumshee.ie

Dear Emma,

Sorry about not communicating much. You're right — it's hard when I'm just lying here, not able to do anything. I've heard nothing yet, and Dad looks terrible.

Anyway, here's my assignment about Sydney.

The beach I usually go to is called Mona Vale. It's pretty quiet, with great surf. By the way, speaking of surfing, if you get a choice of surf gear choose Billabong or Rip Curl. They're the best.

I've never been to the Sydney Opera House, but I do often go to a cinema called Greater Union, in Macquarie (a suburb of Sydney). As for music, none of my crowd are into Oasis. We like Radiohead, Foo Fighters (I don't usually admit to this one in case I get large volumes of hate mail), and The Verve.

I'm in Year 10 at high school and I study English, Maths, Science, Drama, Commerce and History. As for homework, we call it meaning-less drudgery :-) and we do as little as possible. Mostly I play computer games when I'm supposed to be doing my homework. That's the great thing about Windows — you can always

Chapter Twelve

flash back to an English essay if your
mother comes into the room!

That last chess move was pretty clever of
you. I thought you'd do f6 x e5. Of course,
it would have been fatal if you had! Anyway,
what do you think of this?

19   e1 x d1

All the best,

Bruce

CHAPTER THIRTEEN

Emma was really sorry when the last day of term came. In the autumn, she and Orla and the rest of their class would be going to secondary school, in the town. Some of them were on the verge of tears.

'I'm scared of going to secondary school,' confessed Orla. 'Do you know, there'll be about three hundred girls there. Just imagine!'

Emma nodded. She didn't like to say that her primary school in London had been more than twice that size.

She had given up talking about London; in fact, she hardly ever thought about it any more. Secretly, she was quite looking forward to going to secondary school. It would be great fun on the bus, with everyone laughing and telling jokes and swapping homework.

When she got home, her father was waiting for her at the door. He was obviously excited about something; he was rocking backwards and forwards and rubbing his hands together. Emma looked at him hopefully.

'Well,' he said, 'the lines have been busy today. I've had the Sydney police on-line, and the area manager of the bank where Bruce's father works. You won't believe this, but he actually said "G'day" to me, just like that fellow on the TV — what's his name?'

'Paul Hogan, I think,' said Emma impatiently. 'Anyway, go on, tell me. What's happening?'

'Well, nothing yet, but your dear father has landed himself a nice little job from the bank. They're going to e-mail me all the relevant bits and pieces, and they're going to pay me to sort out the whole thing for them. This area manager doesn't really believe that Bruce's father took the money. He's known Mr McMahon for a long time — they play golf together — and he just can't imagine him doing such a thing. He says he'll do anything he can to get Bruce's father cleared.'

'How long will it take you to go through the files?'

'Impossible to tell. It could take days, even weeks, or I could strike gold on my first try. I asked to look at the security log first, so it'll be coming through any moment now. Do you want to come in and have a look?'

Emma nodded eagerly. 'I'll just take Heidi for a quick run, and then I'll make us tea and sandwiches and bring them in.'

As Emma put the tray on the table in her father's study, the e-mail started to download. They both sipped their tea and munched their sandwiches without saying a word.

Emma felt terribly tense. Won't it be awful, she thought, if Dad can't help! After all, the people over in Sydney couldn't find anything wrong ....

The e-mail seemed to take forever to download, but finally it was done. Steve sat down at his desk, opened the file and peered at the screen.

Emma put her cup on the table. She hadn't finished her tea, but it tasted bitter and too strong. She stood at her father's shoulder and peered at the screen. The column of figures and symbols and letters went on and on and on.

After about ten minutes, Steve grunted. 'Funny,' he said. 'Someone's given a chess tuition game the highest priority.'

'What does that mean?' Emma asked.

'If you try to run too many things at once,' her father said, frowning, 'this chess game will still run, no matter what else has to close down to let it keep going. Normally, this area would just be for the operating system. It's a bit odd to have a game in here at all, let alone giving it the highest priority.'

'Why on earth would anyone do that?' said Emma, her excitement mounting. 'This might be that thing you were talking about — the back door!'

Steve grunted again, but said nothing. His eyes were fixed on the screen and his finger was pressing steadily on the mouse, scrolling down. Then he stopped, went back, and scrolled down again.

Emma held her breath. This must be it, she thought.

But her father shook his head.

'Nothing wrong with it, as far as I can see,' he said. 'It's a straightforward tuition game — just chess moves.'

'But it must mean something,' cried Emma. 'What's it doing there, right in the middle of the security files?'

Steve shrugged his shoulders. 'It's not all that unusual,' he said. 'Programmers do all sorts of daft things to give themselves a break when they're programming. Once, when I was going through a very complicated database program, I came across a game called "Lord of the Realm". It didn't mean anything — just that the programmer liked playing it and forgot to erase it from the files before he passed them on to the company.'

'It must mean something,' said Emma stubbornly. 'Here, let me have a look. Keep it still; don't scroll until I tell you to.'

In her mind, Emma went through the game. It was OK for the first ten moves — a fairly straightforward queen's gambit opening — but after that she began to get a bit lost. It didn't seem to make sense.

'Hang on a minute, Dad,' she said. 'I'll just get my chess set and go through it. There's something very odd here. I must have lost track of something, because it looks like he's making an illegal move.'

Emma rushed out of the study, almost falling over Heidi, who was waiting patiently outside the door. She dashed into her own room, seized the chess set, and ran back into the study. Kneeling on the floor, she set up the board and took the pieces through their opening moves, glancing at the screen now and again to check that she was right.

When she came to the eleventh move, she stopped. She stared at the board and then at the screen.

'It's wrong,' she said. 'The game is wrong. He's making an illegal move. Look — he moves his queen, but his king is on the same diagonal as the queen, so when he does that, his king is exposed to check from the black bishop. He can't do that. But he does, and the game just carries on.'

'Go through it again, just to be sure,' said her father slowly.

Emma went through the game again, but it worked out just the same. An illegal move was made, and yet the game carried on.

She stared at her father, her face pale with excitement. 'I'm sure,' she said. 'It's definitely wrong.'

Steve's face was tense and excited as he rapidly scrolled through the program, but then he looked disappointed.

'Oh, hang on,' he said. 'Something's coming up. It's probably some kind of subroutine, a message telling you that you're breaking the rules.'

'Yes, but, Dad,' said Emma impatiently, 'I told you. The game carries on as if nothing's happened. You just can't do that in chess.'

'OK, OK. I'll have a look at the program code for it.'

There was silence for the next ten minutes. Emma opened the door of the study and allowed Heidi to steal in. She sat on the floor, teasing out pieces of goosegrass from Heidi's coat.

'Ah, that's a bit naughty,' said her father eventually. 'They're going into reserved memory space.'

Emma looked up hopefully. 'Into what?'

'Bits of information that no one's allowed to mess with,' said her father absently. He went on muttering to himself. 'I wonder what's kept in this memory space. Let me see .... Check the specification ....'

There was a tense silence. Then Steve jumped to his feet, his voice cracking with excitement.

'Got him!' he shouted. 'We've found our back door, Emma! Between us we've got him! Come and have a look.'

Emma leaped up and peered over his shoulder again.

'This is where the passwords, the usernames, and the users' identities are stored,' said Steve. 'The thief got in here, found Mr McMahon's password and

username, and used them to take the money out of the account.'

'But how did he get in?' Emma asked. 'I don't really understand yet.'

'It was the chess game,' said Steve. 'Forcing the computer to play on after an illegal move was the key that let him into that subroutine, which led into the top-secret part of the reserved memory space. And even if anyone at the bank discovered the chess game, they wouldn't force the computer to make an illegal move and then play on.'

'And of course,' said Emma excitedly, 'it's easy enough to force the computer to make any move; all you have to do is change sides, change from playing black to playing white.'

'Exactly,' replied her father. 'Every chess tuition game lets you do that.'

'So that's it, then,' said Emma, hardly able to believe that they had solved the mystery.

'That's it,' said Steve buoyantly. 'Between us we've cracked it! I would never have found it if you hadn't spotted that discrepancy in the chess game. We'll have to go into partnership, you and I.'

Sydney,
Australia

Dear Mr Mantel,

I am more grateful than I can possibly say for your brilliant work in clearing my name. My reputation is immensely important to me, and I can honestly say that I was nearing desperation when you came up with the solution to the mystery. Please thank your daughter Emma for her help as well. It was very clever of her to find the error in the chess game. I'm afraid I am still a bit hazy about the details, but the outcome is wonderful.

We will be spending Christmas and New Year's Day in Ireland. We have rented a house belonging to a family called McGrath, in Oaghty, near you. Bruce found it on the Internet and fixed everything up in a couple of hours. I really must learn about computers!

Anyway, perhaps when I see you face to face I will be better able to express my profound thanks.

Yours most sincerely,

Daniel McMahon

From: bruce.mcm@clubi.com.au
To: emma@drumshee.ie

Dear Emma,

Yes!!! Very, very, very neat! I don't
know how you and your dad managed to get it.
Isn't it a good job that you knew how to
play chess — and, of course, were good
enough to follow the game in your head!

They've caught the fellow who did it. I
never liked him. He was an awful show-off,
always trying to prove what a great chess
player he was.

Apparently he did work for the firm which
designed the software. The police think he
planned the whole fraud years ago and then
waited a while, just to be safe, before
looking for a job in the bank. Let's hope he
gets a good long sentence. When I think of
what he put my father through, I could murder
him with my own hands!

Has your dad told you that we're all coming
to Ireland for Christmas and the New Year?
I'm really looking forward to it. We get our
long school holiday then — we have the whole
of January off.

To be honest, I think my mother wanted to go
over to Ireland as much as I did. She's
really worried about my father. It's had an
awful effect on him, all this business. I
don't think he'll ever forget that so many
people believed he was actually capable of
doing such a thing. He wanted to retire, but
my mother talked him out of it. She wants
him to have a holiday first, before he makes
any decision.

In the meantime, we can go on playing chess.
I think you might be going to lose this one,
but never mind. You're up against a master
who now has nothing on his mind but beating

you at chess — and, of course, I am two
years older than you!

Love to Heidi (and to you, of course),

Bruce

From: emma@drumshee.ie
To: bruce.mcm@clubi.com.au

Dear Bruce,

Thanks for the e-mail and all your news. I'm
sorry your father is still depressed. I'm
sure you're right, it wouldn't be a good
idea for him to retire early. He'd just get
bored and miserable.

I won't say thanks for your reply to my
pathetic little move 19 — f6 x e5. I was
hoping that I might still have a chance, and
I kept clinging to the fact that the bishop
backed by the queen was strong. I'm a bit
stunned by your move 20, f5 - h6+. I've a
horrible feeling that there might be more to
it than I'm seeing at the moment! I hope you
don't mind, but I'll have to save my move
for my next e-mail; I just don't have the
time to work it out.

I still can't believe that you're coming for
Christmas and the New Year. The house you're
renting at Oaghty is just across the hill
from us. I know the people who own it. They
have a son about my age, called John. Orla
fancies him. He's very good-looking.

To be honest, I was dreading Christmas. It
was always such fun in London, and I thought
it might be boring here in the country.
That's the trouble with being an only child;
it gets lonely sometimes. Orla's always complaining about the size of her family —
there are six of them — but whenever I go

there I think that they have a lot of fun, even though they do fight a lot.

Mind you, Orla's next youngest sister, Carol, can be a bit of a pain, but the little three-year-old, Una, is gorgeous. I'm mad about her, and the funny thing is, Heidi loves her too. I was at the Nolans' last Saturday, and Una dropped a sausage from her fork onto the floor. Heidi picked it up, and Una just stuck her hand right into Heidi's mouth, took out the sausage, said 'No, Heidi, that Una sausage!' and popped it back into her own mouth!

I got a fright for a moment, but Heidi was as good as gold about it. I couldn't stop laughing when I thought what a fit my father would have had, especially about the baby eating a sausage from the dog's mouth, but none of the Nolans took any notice. They're all really easy-going and really nice.

Orla and I are still great friends. We're having a really brilliant summer. We go surfing together almost every day. In the beginning I kept falling off, but I didn't mind. You're right — it is really exciting, now that I'm beginning to get the hang of it. The beach at Lahinch is gorgeous — a mile of sand and enormous waves.

Oh, I can't believe I forgot to tell you! We *did* discover something in the souterrain after all, and it *is* a sort of treasure! The workmen told Dad that the only things there were some huge old pots. We were quite excited about them, because Mum and Dad reckon that they're very, very old. Dad is going to have an archaeologist come and look at them, but in the meantime Mum has them on the terrace, filled with lilies, and they look gorgeous.

But that's not all. When the workmen were gone, I went down there with a torch and I

Chapter Fourteen

saw a dusty little shelf, right up at the top of the wall. Dad got a ladder and checked it out, and he found an old lead box with very strange patterns on it. Inside was a gold necklace, and a piece of paper which said 'This is my mother's gold necklace. It must stay in Drumshee forever, or bad luck will follow.' It was signed 'James McMahon' — he was the old man who sold the place to Dad. He's dead now, unfortunately; he died in an old people's home soon after he sold the farm.

Dad said I can keep the necklace. He's going to get it valued someday, 'when he gets around to it' (that's his favourite expression).

Write back soon.

Love,

Emma

🖳

From: bruce.mcm@clubi.com.au
To: emma@drumshee.ie

Dear Emma,

That's great about the necklace! I think it was in the McMahon family for a long time. My dad remembers hearing about it. He thinks it was originally found in the souterrain. That's probably why James McMahon put it back there before he went into the old people's home.

I've come out of traction — at last! It's such a relief. Please, please, please write back soon. I'm just so bored. Mind you, you're driving me mad telling me about surfing! Don't tell me any more about it. It's bad enough when my friends come to see me. The word 'surfing' is banned in my presence for the next six months.

Tell me about Heidi instead. I'd like to know how she's getting on. I think she must be a very nice dog, really, to let a kid take a sausage out of her mouth. We had a terrier when I was little, and he'd have taken the hand off anyone who did a thing like that.

I'm really looking forward to Christmas and New Year. In a way, Christmas in Australia is a bit of a fake — all that pretend snow and reindeer, and the temperature usually about 95 degrees in the shade. We usually spend it on the beach, but as I won't be able to do any <banned word!>, it would just be a bore. You're right about being an only child. Parents are a bit of a dead weight, when you're the only one to carry the burden.

Hurry up with your next chess move. I have it all worked out.

Love to all. Tell Orla I'm looking forward to meeting her.

Bruce

From: emma@drumshee.ie
To: bruce.mcm@clubi.com.au

Dear Bruce,

20   g8 - h8

That's all I can do, I know, but I still don't see why you're so sure you're going to win.

Anyway, on to Heidi, and staying far away from the subject of <banned word>! I saw an ad in the *Clare Champion* — that's the local newspaper. It had been put in by a guard (that means policeman here) who wanted to know if anyone was interested in doing working-dog trials — tracking and so on — with their dogs. I rang up, and Dermot (the guard running the classes) seemed really nice, so I went along.

The first half-hour — well, let's not go there. I'll just say that 'bad' wasn't the word for Heidi — she was *atrocious*! She barked at every person and at every dog. And most of the other dogs were very well-trained.

The obedience part was a disaster — well, obedience isn't exactly Heidi's thing .... But when it came to working a track, she was actually quite good. I had to leave her tied up — she howled the place down, of course — and then walk through this field of black-thorn bushes and clumps of briars, and hide her bone about a hundred and fifty metres away. When I untied Heidi, she just zoomed along — I thought I'd never manage to hold on to the line coming from her tracking harness, she was going so fast. I also thought she was doing it all wrong, because she didn't seem to be putting her nose to the ground the way the other dogs did. But she found the bone in about two seconds!

The trainer was very impressed. He says Heidi's a natural tracker and that she's an air scenter, not a ground scenter. (Apparently ground scenters just follow the scent on the ground, from bruised grass and leaves and stuff like that, but a good air scenter can follow an air scent as well as a ground scent. Dogs like that can even tell if a particular person has passed by on a bike!) He says I should just let her be the boss. That works OK for me — she's such a bossy dog anyway that it's the easiest thing to do! I must get her to behave herself around other dogs, though. She's getting better with people, but she's still a pain with any dog she doesn't know.

In the first half-hour I almost made up my

mind not to go again, but now I'm determined
to keep going. I'll have to stop myself getting so tense; I think that makes Heidi worse.

How's your leg?

Love,

Emma

🖳

'Bruce said to tell you he's looking forward to meeting you,' Emma told Orla as they walked Heidi and
Tinker up the Togher Field.

'I'm really looking forward to meeting him,' said
Orla. 'I bet he's so, *so* good-looking.'

'Not as good-looking as John McGrath,' teased
Emma.

Orla tossed her head. 'I don't take any notice of
John McGrath,' she said firmly.

'Oh yeah?' said Emma. 'You were taking plenty of
notice of him on the bus the other day. I heard him
asking you if you were going to the disco in Lahinch
on Saturday.'

'Well, that's no good, anyway,' grumbled Orla.
'My mam and dad won't let me go. They say I'm too
young.'

'I know, mine are the same. Anyway, come into
the *cathair* and see what my dad's been doing.'

Steve had bought a big petrol-driven brush-cutter
and cut down all the blackthorn bushes and briars in
the fort. Orla looked around admiringly.

'It looks great,' she said. 'I never realised the *cathair*
was so big. And you can see everything now — all
the hills around. Look, you can see Oaghty over there.'

'Just where a certain John McGrath happens to live,' teased Emma. She looked around the fort. It did look great. Apart from the big pile of branches and briars in the centre, waiting to be burned, everything was neat and tidy.

'Dad's doing all the jobs that Mum's been nagging him to do for months,' she added. 'You see, Bruce's dad's great-grandfather came from Drumshee, and Dad knows that the first thing Mr McMahon will want to do is walk around the farm and see all the places. Do you know, Dad's even had the old cow cabin re-roofed, and it's plastered inside and has new windows and doors. Come down and see it. Mum's thinking of turning it into a guest-house next summer, so we can have friends over. There's loads of room for a big bedroom and a bathroom and a little sitting-room as well.'

'It's brilliant,' said Orla, when she saw the cow cabin.

Emma looked around. The newly painted white walls, and the sunlight streaming through the new windows and skylights, had transformed the place. It did look brilliant. An idea suddenly came to her.

'I've had a brainwave!' she said. 'What about having a New Year party here? I'm sure Mum will say yes. Bruce will be here, and we'll invite all the kids — John and Sophie and Deirdre and Brendan —'

'Yes, and Fiona and Judith and Enda and Edel .... And we can decorate the place!'

'We've got plenty of holly and loads of ivy in the little wood next to the cottage. Oh, and I know what else! I noticed it the other day. There's a big bunch of mistletoe growing on top of that old oak tree. We can hang that in the middle of the room!'

They looked at each other and giggled.

'Not in the *middle* of the room,' said Orla. 'Right in the very darkest corner!'

They giggled again.

🖥

From: emma@drumshee.ie
To: bruce.mcm@clubi.com.au

I can't believe that summer is over and we're all back in school again. I'm glad your leg is so much better, even though I'm sure all that physiotherapy must be a real pain. Still, at least you're back home and able to go to school again — even if you do have to hobble around.

I'm glad you like the idea of the party. Orla and I keep talking about it and planning everything. Dad has got electricity put into the cow cabin — I thought we might have to make do with candles, but he said we might as well get electricity put in now rather than wait for the summer.

We'll have to start another chess game one of these days. When your twenty-first move came in and I saw I could take your queen in exchange for my bishop, I was going, 'Has he finally blown it?' And then I saw your evil little plan. I filled in the position in my chess notebook and sat there staring at it for hours. I couldn't do anything except take the queen, though, and when your next move arrived I knew the only thing I could do was resign. Obviously, if I'd taken your knight with my rook, you would just have brought down your rook from d1 and check-mated me; and if I'd moved my king to g8, you'd have taken my queen and I'd have been a knight and two pawns down, including your pass pawn, which you could easily have queened. So I hadn't a hope.

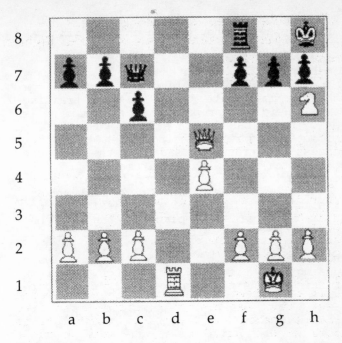

WHITE:	Bruce McMahon, Sydney, Australia		
BLACK:	Emma Mantel, Drumshee, Co. Clare, Ireland		

1	e2 - e4	e7 - e5	13	d4 - f5	e7 - f6
2	g1 - f3	b8 - c6	14	c3 - g3	d7 - e5
3	f1 - b5	g8 - f6	15	c1 - f4	d8 - c7
4	0 - 0	d7 - d6	16	a1 - d1	a8 - d8
5	d2 - d4	c8 - d7	17	d1 x d6	d8 x d6
6	b1 - c3	f8 - e7	18	f4 x e5	d6 - e5
7	f1 - e1	e5 x d4	19	e1 x d1	f6 x e5
8	f3 x d4	c6 x d4	20	f5 - h6+	g8 - h8
9	d1 x d4	d7 x b5	21	g3 x e5	c7 x e5
10	c3 x b5	0 - 0	22	h6 x f7+	
11	d4 - c3	c7 - c6			
12	b5 - d4	f6 - d7			

It was a great game, though. I almost don't want to play another one in case it isn't as good.

Somehow I'm not as interested in chess any more, anyway. All the time I can spare from school seems to be taken up with training Heidi. Heidi — prepare for a shock — is really not a bad dog at all, these days. She absolutely adores tracking. When I put her harness and tracking lead into the car, she starts barking with excitement, and she keeps barking all the way to Corofin, where the classes are held. She drives Dad cuckoo. I've tried hiding the harness — I even put it in the spare-tyre place in the car, but she still smelled it and tried to dig it out! That didn't go down well with my dad, who's very proud of his car and is always fussing about it. I think, though, that the tracking is using up a lot of Heidi's spare energy, so she has a lot less energy left for being bad. I took her into Ennis the other day and she was as good as gold. I was really proud of her.

Love,

Emma

CHAPTER FIFTEEN

It was pouring rain on the day when Emma and her father went to meet the McMahons at Shannon Airport. The aeroplane was nearly half an hour late, and Emma spent most of the time wandering in and out of the washroom and inspecting herself in the mirror. She had a new dress for the occasion; it was a lovely shade of deep purple, with a Celtic motif embroidered on it, and Emma thought it made her look very grown-up. She had also had her long blond hair trimmed at Peter Mark by a girl called Linda, who looked like one of the Spice Girls and who cut Emma's hair so well that it looked bouncy and very fashionable.

She tossed her head, admiring the way that her hair swung, and examined her face carefully in the mirror. She had wondered about lipstick, but her mother had advised against it.

'You're very welcome to buy one if you like,' Joyce had said. 'But if I were you, I wouldn't bother. You're beautifully brown. I think if you put on lipstick, you'll look like a little girl trying to look grown-up. He knows how old you are, so just concentrate on looking good.'

Emma smiled at herself. She thought that she did look good — or maybe it was just a flattering mirror.

At that moment she heard Bruce's flight being announced. She ran out to stand beside her father in the Arrivals Hall.

Emma knew Bruce the moment she saw him. He was even taller than she had imagined, but otherwise he looked just like she had expected him to: deeply tanned, blond, blue-eyed and carrying a surfboard. He was even better-looking than anyone on *Neighbours*.

'Wait till Orla sees him,' she whispered to her father. 'She'll go bananas.'

She moved forward and then stopped, feeling a little uncertain. Bruce did look much older than she had imagined. Maybe he would think she looked younger than he had expected. Maybe she should have worn that lipstick, after all .... She hung back behind her father, smiling nervously.

The journey had given Mrs McMahon a splitting headache, so it was left to Steve Mantel and Daniel McMahon to make conversation. They shook hands and made polite comments about the journey, but somehow they both seemed nervous and ill at ease. Aren't they silly, thought Emma, beginning to feel more self-possessed. You'd think they would have more sense, at their age!

She shook hands with Mr and Mrs McMahon and then with Bruce. The grownups went over to the car-hire desk, and Emma and Bruce were left staring at each other.

'How's your leg?' Emma asked politely.

'Fine.' Bruce seemed a little nervous, too.

'Is it well enough to go surfing?' asked Emma.

'Oh, don't you start!' said Bruce. 'I've had that the whole way from Australia. "Betty, surely that boy's leg isn't strong enough to go surfing." "Do you really think it was a good idea to lug that great big surf-board across the world with you, son?"'

Emma laughed. He had done a very good imitation of his father. Suddenly she felt completely at ease with Bruce.

'Your dad sounds just like my dad,' she said. 'He drives me mad, fussing about things all the time.'

'Where's Heidi?' asked Bruce. 'I was looking forward to her creating a bit of fun at Shannon airport.'

Emma looked around. 'I'll go and get her,' she said. 'She's out in the car. Our parents haven't even got to the top of the queue yet. I'll be back in two minutes.'

She ran out to the car, opened the tailgate and snapped Heidi's lead onto her collar. Heidi was delighted to see her; she pranced around, looking to see if there were any other dogs about.

'Now, for goodness' sake, behave yourself,' said Emma severely. 'Come on, we're going to meet Bruce.'

Her excitement must have shown in her voice. Heidi barked wildly and dashed through the automatic doors, towing Emma after her. Several people drew back nervously, but Heidi stormed on, until she met Bruce, who was coming towards them with a huge grin. Heidi sniffed his hand, wagged her tail and then reared up to plant her front paws on his chest.

'She's great!' said Bruce. 'Get down, you monster, you're going to knock me over. Isn't she friendly?'

'She never is straightaway, normally,' said Emma, puzzled. 'Maybe she smelt my smell on your hand.'

Then she blushed — it had been a stupid thing to say — but Bruce wasn't taking any notice. He had started to play with Heidi, and she was getting more and more excited. Emma noticed that she was the only dog in the airport. Maybe there was a rule against it.

'I'd better put her back in the car,' she said. 'Dad will have a fit if he sees her. We're going to drive ahead of you, to show you where your house is, and then we're going to leave you to have a sleep. Margaret McGrath, the woman you're renting the house from, has done you some baking for tonight, and you're all coming over to us for lunch tomorrow. You'll see Heidi then.'

'How did you get on with Bruce, then?' asked Steve as they pulled out of the airport.

'Great,' said Emma happily, turning back to make sure that the hired car was following them. She waved, and the McMahons waved back.

The next day, Emma was no longer nervous about meeting Bruce. She wore her jeans and sweatshirt, and she never thought about lipstick once. The few minutes of conversation at the airport had been enough to turn their virtual relationship into a real one. Emma felt as comfortable with Bruce as she did with her school friends, and they chattered without stopping all through lunch.

After lunch, while they were loading the plates into the dishwasher, Steve turned on the news.

'We'll get a good weather forecast just after this,' he explained, 'and then you'll know what to expect for the week ahead.'

'It'll probably rain,' said Emma. 'It usually does.'

She didn't care, though. She knew she was going to have a great time. In a couple of days it would be

Christmas, and then there would be the New Year party ....

She was happily clearing the table when her father shouted her name.

His face was white with shock. He was staring at the television set, which showed a familiar scene. Emma recognised it instantly; it was Lemeanah Castle, on the edge of the Burren, only a few miles from Drumshee. Usually it was deserted, but now it was full of people, people looking shocked and bewildered — and among them were Orla and her parents. Mr and Mrs Nolan looked frozen with despair, and Orla was crying. In the distance were three or four policemen, with tracker dogs, their noses to the ground; Emma spotted Dermot, the guard who ran the dog-training classes.

'What's wrong?' she asked. 'What's happened?'

'It's the Nolans' youngest child,' said Steve. 'The little girl called Una. Apparently they all went out to the Burren early this morning, to pick holly, and she strayed away and got lost. They've been searching for her for hours.'

'Oh, no,' said Emma in a despairing whisper, sinking down on the couch. 'Oh, no, not Una.'

'Shhh,' said her father.

The camera had focused on one of the policemen. The microphone was held in front of him.

'Any news yet?' asked the interviewer.

The policeman shook his head. He seemed almost unable to speak.

'But you haven't given up hope?' persisted the interviewer.

At that the policeman found his voice. 'We certainly

haven't given up hope,' he said harshly. 'But it will be dark in a few hours.' He added, almost reluctantly, 'This is a very difficult track for the dogs. A tiny child like that leaves a very small impression on the ground. The dogs find it hard to pick up her trail. And of course, in this rain, any trace on the ground soon gets washed away.'

Suddenly Emma jumped to her feet.

'Dad, I have to go out there. I'll take Heidi.'

'Don't be ridiculous, Emma,' said Steve sharply. 'What's the point of taking that wild, half-trained dog? You heard what the policeman said: it's too difficult even for the real police dogs.'

'No, but, Dad,' argued Emma, 'you don't understand. You don't know about tracking. Heidi is an air scenter — all those dogs are ground scenters. You could see they had their noses to the ground. Heidi would have a better chance than any of them. She's already beaten one of them at tracking, on a rainy day.'

'And Heidi knows Una,' Bruce put in. 'Wasn't she the one you were telling me about, the little girl who took a sausage out of Heidi's mouth? Give it a chance, Mr Mantel. The police can always say no. Dad and I will come too, won't we, Dad? If the police decide to call off the dogs, they'll need all the people they can get to join in the search. They'll have to find her before dark.'

'That makes sense, Steve,' said Joyce. 'Let's give Heidi a chance. I'll come too. What about you, Betty? You must be still tired after that journey. Would you rather stay here?'

'No, I'll come as well,' said Bruce's mother resolutely. 'Lend me a pair of wellies. I couldn't rest thinking of a three-year-old out there in the wet and the cold.'

They all went out onto the porch and began sorting through the collection of wellies in the corner. They were talking in low, shocked voices, but Emma took no notice. Even Bruce hardly mattered now. Her whole mind was centred on finding Una. And everything depended on Heidi.

Emma took down the harness, the lead and the tracking line. She wasn't sure whether to use the short lead or the twenty-metre tracking line. She would have to rely on Dermot to tell her which was best. Heidi was usually better with the tracking line. It gave her more freedom to go her own way, and that always suited her.

I'll put on the harness now, thought Emma. It'll save time if she's ready when we arrive.

Usually Heidi was a pain when Emma put on her harness — she would wriggle, squirm, bark and lick Emma's face — but today she stood like a rock as Emma worked each of her front legs into the harness and fastened the buckles under her chest.

Emma snapped the lead to the back of the harness, and then changed her mind. She wouldn't even ask Dermot. She knew Heidi better than anyone else did, and she was certain the line would be best. She was going to have to rely on her own judgement, and trust Heidi absolutely, if they were to find Una before darkness fell.

It was 23 December, and the sun would set before four o'clock in the afternoon. There was dangerously little time left.

CHAPTER SIXTEEN

There wasn't a sound out of Heidi on the way to Corofin. She seemed to be almost holding her breath, listening to the subdued conversation from the front of the car.

They parked beside the ancient, ruined castle. There were a lot of people there; Emma recognised several of their neighbours, but she took no notice of any of them. Leaving Heidi in the car, she climbed onto a stone wall and screamed 'Dermot!' at the top of her lungs. Several heads turned, and, to Emma's relief, she saw Dermot making his way towards her. She knew she shouldn't interrupt him on a track, but she could tell from the half-hearted way Sabre was circling around that the dog had lost the scent.

'Dermot,' she said, as he reached her, 'could I let Heidi try? She knows Una.'

Dermot shook his head. 'It's no good, Emma, we've been over and over it. We've gone miles. The conditions are too bad; the dogs just can't pick up the scent. I'm about to call them off. And you know Heidi is only a beginner.'

Emma could see that he was very tired. The sweat was running down his face, and there were tight lines of exhaustion around his mouth. From the corner of her eye she could see her father coming towards them — probably full of apologies, she thought irritably.

'But you know she's an air scenter,' she said

rapidly. 'You said that yourself. Surely today, in the rain, an air scenter will do better than a ground scenter.'

There was a silence while Dermot looked at her.

'Oh, go on, Dermot,' Emma pleaded. 'Just give me fifteen minutes. It'll take that long to get these people organised into searching groups, anyway. You can watch Heidi. You know how she tracks: if she's on the scent, her tail will go up so you can see the light-coloured plumes, and then you'll know she's really tracking something.'

Dermot sighed and nodded. 'OK, then. Fifteen minutes. I'll call the other dogs off; that'll give her a chance to concentrate. You've got her dressed and ready — great. I'll just go tell the other lads. We've got the little girl's glove, and you can let Heidi sniff that and see if you can get her to understand. I don't think it'll work, though, Emma. She's never done anything like this before.'

Although she hated doing it, Emma forced herself to walk over to where Orla stood, sobbing, with her father's arm around her. 'Orla,' she said awkwardly, 'I'm going to try Heidi.'

Orla tried to speak, but she couldn't. Emma felt the tears well up in her own eyes, but resolutely she blinked them back.

'Thanks, Emma,' said Mr Nolan. 'Thanks for coming to help.'

'Do you want me to come with you?' gulped Orla, with a great effort.

Emma shook her head. 'No,' she said gently. 'You stay here. You're tired out. Heidi and I will do our best.'

She looked down at the dog's golden head. Heidi had mostly tracked Emma herself, or other people at the classes, but she had also tracked Orla sometimes when they played in the fields at Drumshee. Somehow Emma had to get it through to Heidi that she was going to look for Una.

The big amber eyes were watching her with a slightly worried look. Heidi was puzzled. This was not like ordinary tracking days.

Emma took a deep breath. 'Where's Una, then?' she said, keeping her voice as steady and calm as she could.

A look of comprehension flashed into Heidi's eyes. She looked behind the Nolans, scanned the crowd, then turned and sniffed the small glove that Dermot was holding out to her. She looked over at the field; then, in a flash, she was over the wall and moving purposefully down the field towards a clump of hazel bushes. Emma followed, keeping a steady grip on the middle of the line and leaning back slightly, just as Dermot had taught her. She heard the sound of footsteps behind her.

'You'd better go back, Bruce,' she said, without taking her eyes from Heidi's golden head. 'You might hurt your leg.'

'Blow my leg,' said Bruce. 'Am I in the way?'

'No, but don't talk, and keep behind me.'

At the hazel copse, Heidi faltered for the first time. She cast around uncertainly.

'Find Una, then,' repeated Emma steadily, trying to put a note of confidence into her voice. She blocked out of her mind any possibility that Heidi might fail.

'She'll give you a sausage,' she added. Heidi did know the word 'sausage', and she adored sausages almost as much as she did chocolate biscuits.

Perhaps it was just a coincidence, but at that moment Heidi took off on a new track. She dashed around a rock and under a low-growing tree, where Emma and Bruce had to bend almost double to follow her. With a small thrill, Emma realised that they must be on Una's track. Anyone over the age of six would have gone around that tree, but Una was so tiny that she had just trotted under it.

They moved into a new field, where the going was easier. There was a herd of cows there, but they wouldn't have worried Una; her father had cows of his own, so she was used to them. Emma began to feel a little more hope. Heidi was definitely going somewhere in a very purposeful way. Emma let out some more of the line, taking care not to distract Heidi by jerking it.

Heidi crossed the field, her tail raised like a banner. The rain was falling heavily, but it didn't distract her. She went on as smoothly as a machine, confident and assured, till they reached the edge of the field. Then she stopped, lowering her tail. Emma caught up with her, automatically reeling in the line and looping it around her arm.

She followed Heidi's gaze, and her heart almost stopped for a moment. There below them was a narrow stream, flowing swiftly towards the castle. It wasn't very deep, but it was deep enough for a three-year-old to drown in.

'She did a great track,' said a voice from behind her. It was Dermot, and Emma turned to face him, while Bruce looked wordlessly from one to the other. 'Sabre came here, too,' Dermot went on, 'although the other dogs didn't. I think the little girl wandered

about in that clump of hazels and then came over towards the stream. You'd better come back now, Emma. The other guards are going to search the stream while I organise the neighbours to go through the fields and woodland. Don't say anything to the family, will you, but I think the poor little thing probably drowned.'

Emma nodded, trying to control her tears. She turned to walk back, clicking her tongue at Heidi to make her follow. Suddenly she felt the tracking line tighten. Of course: Heidi, being Heidi, couldn't bear to be beaten. She didn't want to be taken back without finding anything.

'Come along, Heidi,' said Emma, as patiently as she could.

Heidi ignored her and began to nose along the bank. 'Come on, Heidi,' Emma said sharply.

'Oh, Emma, control that dog,' said Dermot over his shoulder, as he strode across the field.

'No, wait,' said Bruce. 'Look, she does look like she's sniffing something along the side of the bank.'

'But no one could have walked there. The bank is too steep,' said Emma, puzzled. 'Look, even Heidi's almost skidding into the water.'

Then, suddenly, a thought struck her. Perhaps Una had walked *in* the water, by the edge of the bank — the water was just about shallow enough at that point. Perhaps she had grabbed at pieces of grass to steady herself, and her wet little hand had left the scent which Heidi was picking up.

Emma said nothing to Bruce. She uncoiled the line and braced herself to follow Heidi. Heidi shot away, so fast that Emma tore her new anorak climbing over some barbed-wire fencing that stretched across the field and through the stream. She didn't hesitate. The first rule of tracking was never to slow down your dog in any way.

Heidi stopped again, and stood looking down into the stream. Emma's heart lurched, and she felt a terrible rush of panic. She couldn't bear to look into the muddy water. Perhaps Heidi had found Una's body ....

Emma began to sob, and her breath came in great gasps. She felt as if she was choking.

'Are you all right?' asked Bruce's concerned voice from behind her. 'Do you want to go back to the car?'

Emma fought to control herself, but she couldn't answer him.

Bruce, however, seemed to understand her terrible fear.

'It's OK, Emma,' he said, giving her a quick hug. 'There's nothing in the water. Are you having an asthma attack?'

Suddenly Emma realised what was happening. It wasn't asthma; she was having another panic attack, just like the one she had had months before. Her mother had explained it clearly to her, and she knew what to do. Carefully she drew in a deep breath and held it until she almost burst. When she was forced to let it out, she immediately took another deep breath.

She was furious with herself. What a childish thing to do, she thought as she held her breath. Everything's depending on me, and then this has to happen.

She was beginning to feel better. It's just silliness, she told herself crossly. You'll be over it in a minute. Now that she was calmer, she could see that there was no sign of Una in the water.

Then Heidi plunged into the stream. It was so sudden that Emma let out her breath in a loud hiccup. She didn't have time to feel embarrassed, though. Without hesitation, she followed Heidi, feeling the water splash over the tops of her wellies and trickle down her jeans. She could hear Bruce splashing after her, but she ignored him.

Heidi was on the far bank, carefully sniffing at branches and bits of grass, then dashing on again. Una must have climbed out of the water.

Emma decided to stay in the stream. She was wet already, and she didn't want to ruin the scent for Heidi. She could hear from the splashing behind her that Bruce had made the same decision. It's great the way we're on the same wavelength, Emma thought.

She felt perfectly calm now. Heidi knows what she's doing, she thought. And Una's a clever little thing. She's used to wandering around farmland and paddling in streams. We'll find her, I'm sure we will.

Near the ruined walls of the ancient castle, the stream turned at a sharp angle, moving away from the castle. Heidi paused and looked around. She seemed to be looking around the fields, but Emma knew her well, and she could see the way Heidi's nostrils were flaring. Heidi was smelling the air.

Dermot, holding a loud hailer, was crossing the field towards them. He stopped and stood very still, signalling to the other policemen to stay away. He knew Heidi, Emma realised, and he knew that her raised tail, with the beautiful pale-gold plumes showing, was a sign that she was still hot on the scent. Emma prayed that Bruce would say nothing. It was important not to break Heidi's concentration.

Suddenly Heidi made up her mind. She looked upwards and then dashed into the castle, towing Emma after her and barking wildly. In through the ruined walls they went, and up the spiral staircase. A quick memory of the sign outside — 'DANGER! NO ENTRY!' — flashed through Emma's mind, but she climbed the steep, broken steps as fast as she could. She could hear Bruce following her. Heidi didn't hesitate for a second; she hardly seemed to feel Emma's weight on the end of the line.

At the top of the spiral staircase, just before the few steps which led out to the roof, there was a small room; and in the far corner of the room a little bundle lay on the floor. Heidi plunged across and began licking it frantically. Una woke up, put two sleepy arms around the dog's neck and said calmly, 'Hello, Heidi, hello, Emma. Where Orla?'

Emma sat down on the floor and picked Una up. She felt like crying again, but she controlled herself. 'Orla's outside, pet,' she said.

Dermot, still carrying his loud hailer, burst into the room. When he saw them, he stopped dead.

'I can't believe it,' he said. 'I was past even praying for this. Good girl, Heidi. Well done, Emma. Wait here.'

In a flash, he was out on the roof, and they could hear him shouting into the loud hailer.

'Mr and Mrs Nolan, your little girl is safe and well. Emma's dog has found her.'

Bruce and Emma looked at each other over the top of Una's curly head. Even through the thick walls of the ancient castle, they could hear the faint sound of cheering.

Emma began to tremble with cold and excitement, and Bruce put his arm around her. He didn't even take it away when Dermot came back in, and Emma didn't really mind. She was beginning to feel almost sleepy, sitting there holding the warm little body.

'What I can't understand is how she didn't hear the loud hailer before,' said Bruce in a low voice.

'Young children are like that,' said Dermot. 'That's why it's especially dangerous to lose them. When they're hurt or frightened, they often just lie down and go to sleep. Give her to me, Emma, and I'll carry her down.'

Heidi, of course, was determined to go first, and for once Dermot didn't insist that she should behave herself. The Nolans, the Mantels, the McMahons and half of Kilfenora met them at the foot of the stairs, and everyone hugged Una and patted Heidi, and all the grown-ups tried not to cry. Orla and Emma didn't even try; they threw themselves into each other's arms and cried their hearts out. They only stopped when they saw flashing lights and realised that they were being filmed by the television crew.

'Just our luck,' muttered Emma, mopping her eyes and blowing her nose. 'It's probably the only time we'll ever be on TV, and here we are with red noses and bunged-up eyes.'

The RTÉ interviewer approached them, and a microphone was thrust under Emma's nose.

'That's a great dog you have there,' said the interviewer. 'How do you think she managed to track the little girl when the police dogs weren't able to?'

Emma took a deep breath. 'Well,' she said, 'I had a lot of help with training her from Mr Nolan and from Garda Collins. Most of the credit should go to them.'

It was a pretty good little speech, she thought. It sounded really grown-up.

Unfortunately, Heidi ruined the effect. She had been eyeing the big fluffy microphone sternly, and suddenly she began to bark wildly and made a lunge at the microphone ....

'Never mind,' said Bruce, afterwards. 'Nobody's perfect, not even Heidi. Now let's get home and fry her up a pound of sausages.'

CHAPTER SEVENTEEN

On the night of Christmas Eve, it began to freeze, and on Christmas Day the Mantels walked to early-morning mass along a road which was white with frost and roofed over with sparkling branches, each twig furred with tiny spikes of ice.

They met the McMahons outside the church. Bruce was wild with excitement. 'Oh, mega!' he kept saying. 'A real white Christmas! How cool!'

'It certainly is *cool*, son,' shivered his father.

Grown-ups' little jokes are so stupid, thought Emma. She smiled warmly at Bruce. 'It's brilliant, isn't it?' she said.

'This will last for a week, at least,' said one of the farmers, when mass was over and the people were wishing one another a happy Christmas. Bruce and Emma looked at each other in delight. Maybe their plan would work after all.

After a huge dinner of roast goose and stuffing and roast potatoes and applesauce and trifle and Christmas pudding, Emma tackled her father.

'Dad,' she began, 'you know that big pile of branches and blackthorn bushes that's been in the middle of the *cathair* for the last few months?'

'I know, I know,' said Steve. He took another sip of brandy and stretched out his legs to the blazing fire. 'I'm going to get around to burning it one of these days,' he said firmly.

'No, Dad, leave it,' said Emma. 'Bruce and I have a

plan. We want to have a huge bonfire up there on New Year's Eve, the eve of the new millennium. You'll be able to see it for miles around. It'll look great. We'll all go up there just before midnight, and on the stroke of midnight we'll all say "Happy New Year!" and sing "Auld Lang Syne" and dance around the fire.'

'Just like they welcomed the new year in the first millennium, in Celtic times,' put in Bruce.

'Won't it be very wet and muddy?' objected Joyce.

'No, it's going to be a fine, frosty night,' said Emma firmly.

'I think it's a great idea,' said Steve warmly. 'Any more brandy, anyone? Betty? Daniel? There's a pine tree blown down by the lane to the old bog,' he went on. 'I'll go down and cut a few branches off it. They'll give a great smell to your bonfire. I love the smell of burning pine,' he added, throwing another log onto the blaze.

'This has been the best Christmas we've ever had,' said Betty McMahon. 'It's been just ....'

'Wonderful,' finished her husband. 'Just like coming home.'

During the next week, while Mr and Mrs McMahon toured the countryside, Bruce, Orla and Emma spent most of their time decorating the cow cabin. They bought a big ball of thick twine, tied holly and ivy to it and hung it along the walls in wide loops. They hung a string of coloured lights from the ancient beam across the centre of the room, and hung the bunch of mistletoe in the corner. Across the end wall was pasted a banner which Bruce and Emma had made on her computer. It was a metre long, decorated with pictures of champagne bottles and clusters of bells. On it was printed, in huge black letters:

millennium@drumshee

By early afternoon on New Year's Eve, everything was ready. All the food was set out on a big trestle table. Joyce had had the week off work and had spent most of it baking cakes and savouries, even though Emma had assured her that most people would just eat chocolates and crisps, and maybe a few cocktail sausages. Still, the cakes and pies and pizzas looked very colourful on their ivy-encircled plates. Joyce had also made an elaborate fruit punch, and although Emma privately thought that most people would be drinking Coke and 7-Up, she did admit that the raspberry punch in its tall glass jug was a glorious sight.

When everything was ready, Bruce and Emma and Orla turned off all the lights except the coloured ones, and Emma went to call her father and mother.

'What do you think?' she asked, as they came in.

'Well, well,' said Steve. 'Just look at the old cow cabin! The cows would never know it.'

'Oh, Dad,' said Emma. 'Stop calling it the cow cabin. Call it the party room.'

'It's great!' said Joyce. 'It looks like a medieval banquet. Did you know there was an old castle here once, Bruce? I suppose this is how they would have celebrated the new year. What's that old carol? Deck the halls with boughs of holly ....'

'You've done a great job, all three of you,' said Steve. 'Let's go up and start the bonfire. There's plenty of wood — no fear of it burning out before midnight. Coming, Joyce?'

'No, I think I'll put my feet up,' said Joyce. 'I'm exhausted.'

Emma lingered behind the others. 'Thanks, Mum,' she said, a little awkwardly. 'Thanks for doing all that for me. I really appreciate it.'

'You have a great time tonight,' said Joyce with a smile, and Emma ran on to join the others.

Steve, with Heidi watching him, was sticking long torches into the ground along the steep path which led to the *cathair*.

'I bought these at a garden centre a few weeks ago,' he said. 'I'll pop out at about quarter to twelve and light them, and then people will be able to see their way up to the *cathair* without tripping over tree roots or anything.'

'My mam and dad are coming at about ten to twelve,' said Orla. 'All the younger ones are coming too. You don't mind?'

'No, I wish the whole world would come,' said Emma happily. 'Anyway, nearly everyone's parents are coming, and their little brothers and sisters, so we should have a great crowd around the bonfire. Thanks for the torches, Dad. It's a super idea.'

By four o'clock the bonfire was burning merrily. Orla went home to wash her hair and get ready for the party, and Emma and Bruce wandered down to have another look at the party room. In the dim, richly coloured lights it looked magnificent.

'I have something to tell you,' said Bruce. 'My father and mother are thinking of buying a little cottage over by Lough Fergus. They'd do it up as a holiday cottage, and maybe move over here in a couple of years, when I've finished my exams. I could go to university in Ireland, my dad says.'

Emma said nothing. It seemed too good to be true. She didn't dare look at Bruce; she turned her eyes up towards the dimly lit ceiling, towards the bunch of mistletoe which hung there.

'Are you pleased?' asked Bruce.

Emma found her voice. 'I'm really pleased,' she said huskily. 'I was dreading you going back, but now I can look forward to you coming again.'

'I know we're a bit young,' said Bruce seriously. 'You are, anyway. You're only thirteen, but you're the nicest, prettiest girl I've ever met. You'll be my girlfriend, won't you? And you'll keep writing to me?'

Emma nodded. 'I will,' she said, and she knew it was a promise she would keep. She didn't feel young. She felt as though she had grown up by years in the past few months.

She looked up at Bruce, and he bent down and kissed her.

'Well, we are under the mistletoe,' he joked, but his face was still serious and he looked very grown-up.

'Bruce, are you coming? I'll take you back to your place now.' It was Steve's voice. Emma heard him slam the car door and reverse around the tight corner by the cottage.

'I'd better go,' said Bruce. 'See you later.'

He ran out. Emma stayed there, standing quite still, under the bunch of mistletoe, until she heard the car trundling down the avenue. Then she switched off the lights and went slowly back into the house.

Joyce was asleep on the couch, and Emma was glad of that. She didn't really want to talk to anyone for a while.

'Come on, Heidi,' she whispered. 'I think you and I should have a little rest too.'

Emma didn't wake up until nearly eight o'clock. In a panic, she washed her hair and ran her bath, throwing in a few capfuls of orange bath oil. When she was out of the bath, her mother came in to help her blow-dry her hair.

'It's been so well cut that it's easy to blow-dry,' said Joyce. 'You must keep going to that girl Linda. I've never seen your hair look so gorgeous.'

Once her hair was dry, it was time for Emma to get dressed. She had persuaded her mother to forget any ideas about velvet party dresses; instead, she had bought a French Connection red top and a black flared skirt, sheer black tights and a pair of red wedge-heeled shoes. She fastened her gold necklace around her neck and whirled around in front of the mirror, admiring the way the pale gold of the necklace matched her hair.

'What do you think?' she asked. 'How do I look?'

'You look like a princess,' said her mother softly.

Outside the cottage, a car door slammed. 'That's Orla,' said Emma. 'She promised to come early. We're going to start the music playing, so everyone can hear it as they come up the avenue.'

Only five minutes after the coloured lights were switched on and a B*witched song had started to spill out into the quiet countryside, a steady stream of guests began arriving, piled into the back seats of cars and vans. The party room began to feel very full.

When Bruce arrived, there was a gasp from most of the girls.

'He's a babe,' Edel murmured in Emma's ear.

'Really *built*,' whispered Sophie, who always prided herself on having the latest trendy expressions.

Bruce danced with Emma for most of the night, but no one minded. Everyone had a partner. The room got hotter and hotter, the bowls of crisps were reduced to crumbs, the bottles of Coke and 7-Up were emptied; even the fruit punch was just a line of red at the bottom of the jug.

Then the door opened and Steve came in.

'Ten minutes to midnight!' he said. 'Put your coats on. It's perishingly cold out there. I hope everyone's brought their wellies!'

They all poured out, laughing and singing, dragging on coats, picking their way in their party shoes over the rough cobbles and exclaiming about the torches flaring beside the path. There was only a curved crescent of a moon, but the velvet blackness of the night sky was splashed with the light of millions of stars. Emma had never seen Drumshee look so beautiful.

A wildly chattering gang, they poured into the *cathair*. It was full of people already; almost all of the parents had arrived. The Nolans were there, with little Una safely in her father's arms; Heidi was beside them, her nose touching Una's foot.

The leaping flames of the bonfire sent black shadows moving on the frosty ground. Emma, holding Bruce's hand firmly, thought that Heidi's shadow seemed like the shadow of a great wolf from long ago, and that the whole *cathair* looked as if it were alive with shadows from the past. She thought about all the people who had lived there through the centuries — the men and women, girls and boys who had lived and laughed and suffered and died within the walls of Drumshee. As the second millennium melted into the third, it felt as if past, present and future had begun to merge.

She looked at the handsome boy beside her and suddenly knew, with absolute certainty, that here was her future. Once again, there would be McMahons at Drumshee.

It was approaching midnight, and Steve Mantel and Daniel McMahon appeared from the souterrain carrying bottles of champagne and trays of glasses. Corks popped. Everyone, even the boys and girls, took a little champagne. Glasses were raised, and as the church bells of Inchovea and Kilfenora pealed out, a great shout rose up from the ancient walls of Drumshee:

'Happy New Year! Happy New Millennium!'

Visit our website at

www.drumshee.com

*for great competitions,
exciting information about the whole Drumshee series
and about the real Drumshee,
and a chance to share your ideas and opinions
with other Drumshee fans everywhere!*

All Drumshee books are available from:
WOLFHOUND PRESS
68 Mountjoy Square
Dublin 1
Tel: (+353 1) 874-0354   Fax: (+353 1) 872-0207